To my dear Granddaughter, Mindy
Grandmother Stoltzfus.

Bittersweet Days

Bittersweet Days

Dorothy Hamilton

Illustrated by
Esther Rose Graber

HERALD PRESS
Scottdale, Pennsylvania
Kitchener, Ontario
1978

Library of Congress Cataloging in Publication Data

Hamilton, Dorothy, 1906-
    Bittersweet days.

    SUMMARY: Marooned with her family in a snowstorm while on a
camping trip, Kathy searches for her inner self, and when she returns to
school, discovers her true friends are not members of the "in group."
    [1. Identity—Fiction] I. Graber, Esther
Rose. II. Title.
PZ7.H18136Bi   [Fic]   77-18867
ISBN 0-8361-1845-6
ISBN 0-8361-1846-4 pbk.

BITTERSWEET DAYS
Copyright © 1978 by Herald Press, Scottdale, Pa. 15683
    Published simultaneously in Canada by Herald Press,
    Kitchener, Ont. N2G 4M5
Library of Congress Catalog Card Number: 77-18867
International Standard Book Numbers:
    0-8361-1845-6 (hardcover)
    0-8361-1846-4 (softcover)
Printed in the United States of America
Design: Alice B. Shetler

10 9 8 7 6 5 4 3 2 1

To
Helen Tirey
and
John Herfel

Chapter 1

Some days Kathy Miller didn't understand her own feelings. This was one of those times. *Here it is Friday evening,* she thought, *and I'm not caring whether anyone calls me. And it doesn't seem important that no one asked me to go to the Sundae Shop after school. I don't get it.*

She sat down on the low chest under the west window of her room and looked across the street, without really seeing anything. Her mind was full of questions. *Why do I feel more mixed up now than I did last year? Is it because of changing schools? Or because I have more friends, or because I don't see Cindy so much?*

All at once she was tired of that kind of thinking. She shook her head and reached for one of the books between the creamy onyx horseheads. *My favorite*, she thought, as she looked at the title. *At least it was for a long time.* She remembered telling her mother over and over, "I wish I'd been born during olden times and could have come to Indiana with pioneers in a covered wagon."

"I understand that feeling," her mother always said. "I used to wish I could have sailed on the *Mayflower*. But it might not have been as much fun as the author would have you think."

Now as Kathy leafed through the book she knew her mother had been right. *I wouldn't have liked everything. But some parts still seem good.*

She heard the ring of the telephone and tiptoed to the door of her room. *It could be for me. Pat, or Val, or maybe even Cindy.*

She listened to her mother's part of the conversation and within two minutes she knew it was her father who'd called. She walked across the hall and sat on the top step. She stretched her legs and rubbed her toes back and forth on the new stair carpet. She liked the bristly feel. *We're going someplace. Mom's already said we can be ready by five if we hurry. I guess I'm not going to have anything to say about whether we go or not. Wayne either.*

With one movement Kathy's mother put the telephone on its cradle and turned to look up. "We're going on a little trip to the southern part of the state.

8

Your father's rented a camper. Come on down and I'll make some lists."

"How'd you know I was sitting here?" Kathy asked in surprise.

"That's easy. You always appear at the first jingle of the telephone."

I'm not quite sure how I feel about going, Kathy thought. Then she realized that this wasn't true. *I truly want to go, but it does look to me like I should have been asked. Not told.*

"This sudden decision is hard on me," Lois Miller said as she took a pad of paper from a top drawer in the maple cabinets. "I like to plan farther ahead than this."

"You didn't say anything like that to Dad."

"I know. He was so excited I hated to spoil things for him. Besides, I know how badly he needs to get away."

"You mean because Uncle Ken pulled out of the business and left Dad with the whole load."

"Yes, and the burden of raising money to pay Ken for his share."

"But how can Dad get away now?"

"Your Grandfather Miller came over from Oakville. He insisted that your father take a couple of days off. So! I'll get the picnic baskets and pack these items. And you run to the grocery for what's on this list."

"How about Wayne? Doesn't he have to do anything?"

"Oh, my goodness! I should have had you call him first. He's playing basketball over at Greg's. Stop by and send him home."

The Millers didn't leave town until a little after five-

9

thirty. It took longer to pack the clothes and food and other supplies than they'd allowed.

"I'm sure we're going off without something we'll need," Kathy's mother said.

"There *are* stores here and there over the state," Rex Miller said. "Are you sure you have matches? There's a gas stove and we may need the heater by the time we stop for the night. Spring weather can be tricky."

"Oh, surely we won't have any really bad storms," Lois said. "After all, it's April."

As Kathy ran back upstairs for her gold corduroy coat she realized that none of her friends would know where she was. *I should have called someone.* She stopped in the hall and dialed Val's number. *Busy! And probably will be for an hour. And there's no use calling Cindy. She's candy-striping tonight—I think.*

Her mother was still in the kitchen. "Look around. Check on me, Kathy. See for sure that I turned off all the burners and locked the windows while I get a couple of books."

"Books? Will we have much chance to read while we're away?"

"I don't know, but I always like to take some reading along."

"Maybe I'd better get something too."

"You'd better hurry. My built-in timer says your father has been patient about as long as he can stand."

Wayne was coaxing to be allowed to ride in the camper when Kathy reached the driveway. "It's against the law, I think," Rex Miller said.

"I see people in them," Wayne said. "Kids peek out windows all the time."

People do a lot of things which are against the law—

all the time. But that doesn't mean we're going to break the rules."

They left town before sunset and were out on the state highway when Wayne said, "Hey! We forgot something. We didn't eat."

"I'm surprised you didn't think of that before," his mother said.

"I didn't have time to remember. What are we going to do anyway?"

"We'll stop at a drive-in. There are some good places on the edge of New Castle," Rex Miller said.

"That reminds me of the new girl in my biology class," Kathy said. "She says drive-ins are dumps."

"That probably doesn't make her too popular," Lois Miller said. "Not with those who live on cheeseburgers and french fries."

"She doesn't seem to care. 'You're all too Midwestern,' she goes."

"Goes? Goes where?" Kathy's father asked.

"She means *said*, Dad," Wayne answered.

"Then why doesn't she say what she means?"

"And while we're on that subject," Lois said. "How can we be too Midwestern? That's what we are—and where we are."

"She means we aren't like her," Kathy said.

"Well, I'd say that's her problem," Rex Miller said. "I'm ready to eat and I'm glad to see the drive-in up ahead. Get your orders in mind."

It was dark by the time they reached Rushville. The moon, a pale gold crescent, was rising from behind the black fringe of trees on the horizon. "Perhaps we should have found a camping place while it was daylight," Lois Miller said.

11

"No problem. A customer has a cousin who runs a campground down a road off the highway. Watch for a sign, "Elm Grove Campground." There'll be a space. I called."

They drove a mile down the Tarvia road which intersected State Road 3 and then turned left. The tree-lined lane was narrow and a little rough. "Are these elms, Dad?" Wayne asked.

"I can't tell in the dark. Besides, I'm trying to miss the chuckholes."

"I doubt if there are this many elms left in one place," Lois Miller said. "Some kind of disease has killed most of them."

Kathy and her mother stayed in the car until the owner led them to their campsite and connected the camper's water hose to a pipe. "How will we see?" she asked.

"There are gas lamps and I put in several candles," her mother replied.

"Come on," Rex Miller said as the campground owner went up the trail. The lantern he carried made bobbing motions as he walked and patterns of light danced ahead and behind him.

"This is great," Wayne said. "Like a little house."

"Chilly though," Kathy said.

"Button your coat until this gas heater gets going," her father answered.

Kathy sat down at the table on one of the padded benches on each side. *Where are we going to sleep?* she wondered.

As she shivered, her father answered part of her question with another. "You want the top bunk, son?"

"Sure."

"Then Kathy can sleep where she's sitting after I put the table out and pull out the seat extensions."

"Are we going to bed *now?*" she asked. "It's not nine o'clock yet."

"I'm going to settle down as soon as all of you will let me," her father said. "Take advantage of all this quiet. No telephone bells. No television. No traffic noise."

"Can't I even listen to my transistor?" Wayne asked.

"If you keep it low."

"I'll do better than that. I just found my earphones. They were stuck in the bottom of the case."

Kathy was yawning by the time everyone else was ready for bed, but she didn't go to sleep for a while. Her father's use of the word telephone reminded her of something she'd tried to ignore. *Didn't Val or Pat or any of the others call me because of Mom's rule? Do they think I'm a drag because of the ten-minute limit?* She reached back for the small square pillow and put it over her ear. *Now why did I do that? There aren't any noises to shut out. I guess it's that one terrible thought I want to get away from. That the kids will talk about me because my parents are sort of strict—like they do other kids—even Cindy sometimes."*

She raised her head and looked out the slanted window at the end of the camper. She couldn't see much except shadows and shapes of trees. A mournful sound made her lie down and cover her head. She felt a tug of the blanket and turned to look up to where Wayne was leaning from the upper bunk. "Did you hear that owl, Kathy?" he whispered. "that's really great."

"To you, maybe," Kathy said. "I think it's mourn-

13

ful. Let me go to sleep. Good night." She was half awake when she had the sensation of being rocked. She raised her head from the pillow and heard the swish of wind through the trees. *It's shaking the camper—it's like that song mothers sing—the one that goes, "When the wind blows the cradle will rock."*

It's funny how one thought leads to another, she thought after she'd pictured the rope swing which hung from the limb of an apple tree on her uncle's farm. *What was the name of those apples? They were so big and not really good to eat.*

The name of the tree came from somewhere in her memory. *Wolf River. Is there a stream by that name somewhere near? I never heard of it. Did that Johnny Appleseed bring the seeds for them from somewhere far away?* She thought she heard the gurgle of running water before she went to sleep. *But that's probably my imagination, because I was thinking about rivers.*

Chapter 2

By ten o'clock the next morning the Millers were ready to leave Elm Grove campground. They'd slept late and no one seemed to be in a hurry either to fix breakfast, or to eat the cereal and scrambled eggs and hot chocolate. As Kathy watched the bubbles float around in her pink flowered mug she asked, "Why aren't we in a big rush to get going?"

"Two reasons," her father answered. "Rushing is the one thing I don't intend to do for these two days."

"And the second reason?"

"I'm not sure where we'll go. So how can I be in a hurry to get there?"

"You don't know where?" Kathy asked.

"Not for sure. But if we find a good campground with recreational facilities we'll stay there until tomorrow afternoon. Or we might hit a state park."

It sounds dull to me, Kathy thought. She felt like saying so. *But everyone else seems to be having a good time. I'd come out sounding like a grouch—a drag.*

They drove southwest for over an hour and a half, stopping only to get a cardboard tub of fried chicken and a pint of potato salad. Before the container was cold they came to a sign pointing to Leisure Acres. They saw that this campground was better equipped than the one in which they'd stayed the night before. "It's more like a park," Kathy's mother said. "There's a playground up that slope."

"And some kind of a recreation hall to the right," Rex Miller said. "This is as good as any we're likely to find in the time we have. Probably better than most."

What will we do here with a bunch of strangers, cooped up in this little camper? Kathy wondered. Then she had to face something about herself. *All these years I've said I wanted to be a pioneer. Now this is a little like it would be to travel by covered wagon— only a lot more comfortable—and I'm complaining!*

By Sunday noon the Millers were thinking about starting north. "I'll pack everything after lunch," Kathy's mother said. "Will we be home in time for dinner?"

"Should be," Rex Miller said. "Is there food left in case we don't, or run into a stretch where places are closed?"

16

"Oh, yes, plenty. Stopping to eat and buy food has been easy on what I brought."

Before they headed home, Kathy played three games of Ping-Pong with her brother in the game room of the recreation hall. Several men watched a pro basketball game on the television set in the center lounge. Lois Miller took a long walk along the river trail which wound alongside the campground.

Kathy went back to the camper before the other members of her family returned. She read three chapters from her book, then stood up and reached for Wayne's radio. She turned the notched black wheel, hunting for a clear station. *There's a lot of static here,* she thought. *Is it because of the tall trees?* Then a voice blared above the crackling, "The weather watch has been changed to a travelers' warning. Heavy snows accompanied by strong winds are sweeping into the state from the west."

I should go find Dad, Kathy thought. Before she could rescue her shoes from under the table, her mother opened the door.

"We're leaving now," Kathy's mother said.

"Because of the weather?"

"You heard then? So did your father. A bulletin came on the television."

"You think we can make it home?"

"Your father is going to try. He says we're headed northeast. The storm's behind us and we should be able to be home by dark if the weather forecaster is right."

They'd been on the road a little over an hour when snowflakes began to float and dance in the silver-gray air. For a while the heat of the motor dried them on

17

the windshield. After that the wiper kept the glass clear until after four o'clock.

"Are we close to home, Dad?" Wayne asked as they came within sight of a small town.

"In good weather we'd make it in an hour or maybe an hour and a half at the most. But this white stuff is getting heavy. It's beginning to cover the highway. Traffic's not keeping it clear."

Kathy sat back in the seat and looked out the window. It was nearly dark and the snow was like a white curtain blowing toward the car. "Seems like we're going slower and slower. And there's a car in the ditch over there. Way down. It's lights are pointing up."

They kept moving for what seemed like much longer than an hour to Kathy. Cars they met were moving slowly. Then she felt a jerk as they slid to a stop. "That camper ran up on us a little," her father said. "As far as the hitch would let it go."

"Why'd you stop right in the middle of the road?" Kathy asked.

"Because cars ahead of us are stopped," Wayne said. He was resting his arms on the back of the front seat and leaning forward. "Can we get out, Dad, and see what's going on?"

"Not yet. The line may move anytime. And we want to be ready to move with it."

The cars ahead did move now and then, but it seemed to Kathy they went forward only by inches. "There's a flashing red light ahead," Wayne said. "A cop, maybe."

"Or an ambulance," Lois Miller said.

Rex Miller rolled down a window as a state policeman stepped from the center line. "What's the trouble?"

"There's been an accident. A semi jackknifed and there's a car pileup."

"Can we get around it?"

"You can—but it's going to be at a snail's pace until wreckers can get through the drifts."

"Drifts?"

"Yes. From here to Muncie and on farther. If you know the country I'd turn off here. The east-west roads are fairly clear."

"I think I'll take that chance," Rex Miller said. "I'm not too far from home."

The tires spun until they took hold. Lois said, "Is this wise? You don't really know this part of the country that well. Or do you?"

"Maybe not. But I didn't want to be tied up in that snarl all night."

The road they took ran straight for a while. Then it curved and headed in a northwestern direction. The snow was deeper and even in low gear it was slow going. "I'm stopping," Rex Miller said. "It's getting worse, and *fast*. I see a woods up there. If there's a lane I'll pull in. The trees will be some protection against the wind."

"We might get stuck," Lois said.

"True. And we may stall right in the road—out in the open."

They nearly missed seeing a gate to the right. The beams of the car light gave them a glimpse of the metal and wire. "Want me to open it, Dad?" Wayne asked.

"Better let me. My shoes are higher and my legs are longer."

19

"I never once thought of putting in boots," Kathy's mother said. "Who would in April?"

Kathy's feelings were mixed. She was both scared and excited. *I don't want to freeze or starve,* she thought, *but it is a kind of adventure. All alone in a wilderness.*

The wind had swept the snow away from the entrance to the woods, and there was some protection from the strong gusts and the swirling snow. Kathy's father pulled the trailer up to its full length then backed so they could walk to it in the tire tracks. "Bring that bag of apples," Lois Miller said. "They might freeze overnight."

The gas heater warmed the camper within a half an hour. "Let me hang all of our coats and sweaters in the closet. We might as well keep things neat. Then we'll decide what we want to eat."

"I'm not too hungry," Kathy said. "Wayne and I got potato chips and peanuts from the vending machines."

"But that was a *long* time ago," Wayne said.

"How about tomato soup?" Kathy's mother said. "I can make toast in this little oven."

"Fine with me," Rex Miller said. "And I'll choose apples for dessert."

"You sure we have plenty of food, Mom?" Wayne asked.

"For a day or so we can manage. We have eggs and cold cuts and cheese and crackers."

Even in low gear it was slow going. "I'm stopping," Rex Miller said. "The snow is getting worse fast."

"And apples," Rex Miller said as he bit into a crisp Red Delicious.

I wonder if Mom and Dad are worried inside, Kathy thought as she placed silverware, napkins, and mugs for the soup on the table. *They wouldn't let us see if they were. At least they'd try not to show it. But sometimes I can tell. Especially by Mom's eyes. They get a little misty—or clouded. And Dad gets to talking faster.*

Snow fell as long as the Millers were awake. Wayne pulled a box of dominoes from his gym bag and coaxed the others to play a game with him, one at a time. "That way I'll get to play longer. If all of you played, Kathy'd quit after getting beaten. She always does—quit and get beaten."

"Well, we all can't be good at everything," Kathy said. "Like you are in math."

She read, lying on one of the couches that could be pulled together to make a double bed. "I'm getting thirsty," she said as Wayne stacked his dominoes in the long and narrow box. "What will we do for water?"

"We can melt snow. That's what pioneers did—and trappers," Wayne said.

"We don't have to do that yet. There are three two-gallon jugs in the storage under that couch. I filled them this morning," Rex Miller said. "This morning! That seems like a long time ago."

"Wonder how long we'll be here?" Wayne asked after he'd climbed the four-rung ladder to his bunk.

"It's hard to say," his father answered. "These late storms don't last long. It's not real cold—not much below freezing. A spell of warm sunshine could change the picture."

22

"A snowplow would be quicker," Lois Miller said.

"It may be awhile before one gets to a back road like this."

"How do you know it's a back road, Dad, if you don't know for sure where we are?" Wayne asked.

"I guess it's back of somewhere."

Kathy thought about several ideas before she went to sleep. None of them were disturbing. *Not once all day have I wondered if Pat or Val or anyone is saying bad things about me. Or if they're ever going to call me or ask me to go to the Sundae Shop. That all seems far away from now.*

She went to sleep remembering the time when she and Cindy were together more than they'd been since entering High school. *We never exactly had a fight or anything, she thought. It was just that we didn't want to go the same places—or be with the same people.* She locked her hands behind her head and looked sideways toward the window. *I guess I'm not being quite honest—again. I'm the one who wanted to go with Val and Pat and sometimes Wendy Larrimore. Cindy never would. But she never said why. Why didn't I make her tell me the reason? Or would I have listened?*

The gas heater sputtered now and then and snow hit the window with soft plops when the wind blew it against the glass. *Why do I feel so safe? Out here—out of contact with everyone—except Mom and Dad and Wayne. Cindy would like being here—I just know she would.*

Chapter 3

Kathy realized that the April storm had ended before she opened her eyes the next morning. She felt the warmth of sunshine on her face. The light was so bright and so white that she blinked several times before raising up on one elbow. Tiny streams of water ran down the glass. *Snow on top of this camper is melting,* she thought. *But there's still plenty on the ground, for as far as I can see.*

"You decided to begin the day?" her mother asked.

"I didn't know anyone else was awake."

"Yes, we have been for an hour or more. Your father and brother are out looking around."

"Won't their feet get wet and cold?"

"Probably. But they put some of the plastic bags— the ones I brought for storing food—over their socks. But I expect to be drying footwear when they get back."

"I don't see how they got dressed and out of here without me hearing them."

"They didn't—dress all the way, I mean. They gathered up clothes and went to the car."

"Do you think we'll get out of here today?" Kathy asked, as she brushed her hair.

"Who knows?"

By the time Kathy had melted snow and scrubbed her face, Wayne and her father were back. Her mother met them at the door. "Take this plastic bucket and scoop up more snow for melting."

"Are the jugs empty already?" Rex Miller asked.

"No. But I want to save that water for drinking and cooking. How far did you go? Do you know where we are?"

"We didn't go far enough for me to get a sense of direction, except I know the road out there goes north."

"How do you know that? Is there a sign?"

"No. But the sun's up. So I know where east is."

As they ate poached eggs on toast Kathy's father told more about their walk. "The air is clear and still. We stopped and listened and didn't hear any signs of traffic. I'll go out again in a couple of hours and try to find out if anything's moving."

"And where we are, I hope," Lois Miller said. "I don't like this lost feeling."

"We're not that lost."

Kathy stepped outside after breakfast, being careful to walk only in her father's footprints. "The world looks beautiful," she thought. Snow and frost whiskered every twig on every branch of the bushes and trees. The sun made everything sparkle. A sifting of cold hit her cheek and she looked up in time to see the flutter of a bird as it darted from one snow-covered limb to another. She turned and giant-stepped back to the camper. "Can we spare something for the birds?"

"I think so," her mother said. "Here are some bread scraps. And some apple peelings. Do you think birds like them?"

"Well, maybe it's like you tell me. If they're hungry they'll eat them, and if they're fussy that's their problem."

"Only I don't say fussy. I say finicky."

"Finicky. That's a funny word. I wonder if it's in the dictionary?"

"I don't know. Probably is. At least it's in my vocabulary."

Without thinking Kathy said, "That's the way it is with a lot of words."

Her mother turned from the sink and lifted her hands from the soapy water. "Something tells me this is a time for listening, listening with a capital L."

Kathy knew what her mother meant. She'd known for a long time that the little girl who grew up to be her mother had been a lonely child. "There were a lot of people at our house," Lois often said. "We lived with my grandparents. And they talked a lot, and had company nearly every day. They even talked to me, but they never listened. Not really. I could tell. What they said was never really an answer. I wanted to scream 'Listen' in capital letters."

"Maybe it is. That kind of time I mean. I'll come in when I scatter this food for the birds."

As Kathy threw scraps into the grove of trees she wished in one way that she hadn't let on how she felt about the kind of words some kids used. *Maybe it's kind of disloyal to talk about it—disloyal to Pat and Val. But they're not as bad as Wendy Larrimore and some others. Not quite.*

"Here's a broom. Brush the snow off your shoes," her mother said when Kathy returned to the camper. "That pigskin takes a long time to dry. Now, I'm listening. Sitting down, even."

Kathy slid into the seat at the opposite side of the table. She didn't know how to go on with what she'd started. "Maybe I shouldn't have said anything about this."

"Why? Because you think I won't understand?"

"No," Kathy said. "It's not *that*. Well, I may as well say it. I'm shocked and embarrassed a lot of the time by what kids say—and the words they use to talk about things."

"Perhaps you should be proud of yourself because you *are* shocked. I'm afraid I'd be disappointed in you if you weren't."

"I know what you mean. And you're right. It's just that—"

"That they ridicule you for not joining in."

"Sometimes," Kathy said. "But mostly they make fun of me for blushing or walking away."

"They used to call me a goody-goody when I was your age," Mrs. Miller said.

27

"They *did?*"

"Yes. A lot."

"What did you do?"

"I suffered a lot. I felt like I was odd, until I found others who were like me. But I think my Sunday school teacher helped me more. She said that filthy or profane language is inaccurate. 'Such words either don't say what people mean or they say nothing at all—so why mess up your mind with them?' is the way Miss Waldo put it. She said they're really signs of stupidity."

"Wow!" Kathy said. "I can see the faces of some kids if I said *that.* One thing they don't want is to be called stupid."

She was ready to ask her mother another question when she heard the car motor start. She looked out and saw puffs of gray-white smoke coming from the exhaust pipe. "What's Dad doing?"

"Probably checking to see if the motor would start."

Wayne came to the door. "We're going to walk in the other direction. See what's over the hill ahead."

"Want some more plastic bags?" his mother asked. "Or maybe the ones you used are dry by now."

"Dad says we won't go far. And the sun's settled the snow. Some places you can walk on top, like we have on snowshoes."

"Then I think I'll go. Want to come, Kathy?"

"Yes. For a little way anyhow."

She and her mother walked where her father stepped until they came to the top of the hill. When they were all standing still they heard the hum and chug of motors. "Look down there," Rex Miller said. "There's State Road 3."

"And a snowplow!" Wayne said. "Two of them."

Kathy saw wide plumes of snow fan out from the heavy scoops.

"Do you know where we are? We're not far from Memorial Park outside New Castle!"

"Are you sure?"

"Yes, I'm positive."

"But we still can't get out," Kathy said.

"No. Not until a plow comes down the side road. But I'm going to go down to the Smith Auditorium after lunch. If they're open I'll call the store and let Dad know where we are. Now that *we* know."

"Could you call someone to send a plow down the back road?"

"Well, I can call the highway barn and ask when they might get here. But we have to realize they can't be everywhere at the time people expect."

"Why are we waiting to go after lunch?" Wayne asked.

"Because I'm getting hungry and my feet are already wet."

Kathy's mother browned cold cuts in butter for sandwiches, and opened the one can of baked beans. As they bubbled, she diced unpeeled apples, celery, and the fourteen tokay grapes they hadn't eaten. "I know there are fourteen," she said. "I cut each in half and figure each of us can have seven pieces."

"Who's going to count them?" Rex Miller said. "You or us?"

"I could as I put the salad on plates," she said as she spooned creamy salad dressing into the bowl. "Each of you is on his—or her—honor not to take more than the proper share."

It was after two-thirty in the afternoon before Kathy heard her father and brother come back to the camper. She had listened to Wayne's radio and fallen asleep for a while. She looked out the window and saw her mother coming from the direction of the side road. She shook her head when she saw Kathy. *That means there's no snowplow in sight.*

"You think we'll be here another night, Mom?" she asked as her mother came inside.

"We may. Of course there are several hours of daylight left. And I suppose snowplows have lights. I'd better see what I can put together for another meal—or two."

Kathy wasn't sure how she felt about being snowbound for another day. She wasn't bored or worried and she couldn't understand why. *At home I'd have been pacing the floor, or tearing my hair, or climbing the walls—or felt like it—if I hadn't seen any of the group or talked to them. Why is it different here?*

When Wayne opened the door he said, "The snowplow's coming."

"Right now? I'd better pack," his mother said.

"No hurry," Rex Miller said. "All the highway superintendent could promise was that the road would be open by dark."

"You called Grandpa?" Kathy asked. "Was he worried?"

"He didn't let on. Said he figured we had sense enough to get in out of the snow."

"How could we? When it's everywhere?" Wayne asked.

"He meant in off the road, I imagine."

They'd finished their evening meal and Kathy and

her mother were repacking the picnic baskets when they heard the roar of the snowplow. "We can go now. Right?"

"We'll have to wait until they go back on the other side," her father said. "But it'll hurry us to get packed up by then."

"Are there any more scraps for the little birds?" Kathy asked.

"In that bread wrapper."

After taking a few steps into the woods Kathy stopped and scattered the pieces of food in all directions. All the snow had melted or fallen from the branches. She could see patches of smoky gray sky. One was decorated by a shimmering star. "Everything's so quiet—so peaceful. Do the birds feel sheltered—like I did last night in the camper?"

"Come on, Kathy," her mother called. "It's time to go now." As she went toward the car Kathy saw clusters of cream white berries on a bush. She broke off a twig and shoved it into one of the deep pockets of her coat. *I'll put it in my treasure frame—to remind me of here.*

As they rode home Kathy thought about the deep picture frame her grandfather had sectioned into little boxes and backed with a mirror. *I haven't put anything in it for a long time, nothing besides the shells and sweet gum balls and chunks of agate and the polished tiger's eye.*

Chapter 4

I'll help unload," Rex Miller said as he turned into the driveway. "Then I'll run this camper over to the sales lot so I won't have to pay another day's rent."

"This is the part of going I don't like," Kathy's mother said.

"You mean coming back?"

"No. The unpacking. It's not much fun."

"I'll help," Kathy said.

"Not if you have homework."

"I probably do, but I don't know what."

"You could call someone."

"Maybe I will," Kathy said, "later."

It was nine o'clock by the time clothes were sorted and either put in the hamper or stored in closets or drawers. Kathy thought of calling Pat or Val but for some reason she didn't want to talk to either girl. *Anyhow, if they want to know where I've been they'd have called here. Could be they didn't even miss me.*

She sank down on the soft leather couch in the heated sun porch and ran one finger along the row of buttons which tufted the camel tan covering. "Why didn't you turn the TV on?" Wayne asked as he came from his room.

"I didn't even think about it. I guess I'm out of the habit. I can't think right now—what's on tonight?"

"I'll see," Wayne said as he clicked the dial. The sound shut out the ring of the telephone and Kathy wasn't aware that anyone had called until her mother said, "It's Cindy."

"Hi," Kathy said as she sat down on the next to lowest stairstep.

"Hi, yourself. When did you get back?"

"Oh, about seven-thirty I think. We've been snow-bound."

"I know. I tried to call Saturday. Then when you weren't at school I stopped by the store. Your grandfather said you were probably caught in the storm somewhere."

"Well, we were. Only we didn't know exactly where until this morning. We walked over a hill and there was Memorial Park. By New Castle."

"I know. Where they have the lake with swans."

"And ducks and gray geese."

"Was it exciting? Did you have enough to eat and keep you warm?"

"Well, I guess I'd have to say yes to all three questions."

Cindy asked if Kathy wanted the history assignment. "That's all I can give you because we're not in any other class together. Or did Pat or Val give them to you?"

"I haven't talked to them."

"Really?"

There's a question in her voice, Kathy thought. *Doesn't she believe me? Or is she just surprised?*

"You still there?"

"Yes. I was thinking," Kathy said. "You didn't sound as if you believed me."

"You mean about not talking to the other girls? It wasn't that. It just didn't seem natural—I mean you're real thick with them."

"Well. Maybe not like you think. I've been sort of mixed up lately. And being away made me see some things." She paused and then added, "I wish it wasn't so near to bedtime. I'd ask you to come over. Could you—or would you want to?"

"Sure. No reason why not except I know what my mother would say. Tomorrow's"

"I *know*," Kathy said. "Tomorrow's a school day. It's time for you to be in bed. Mine would say the same thing."

"She would?"

"Yes. Did you think she wouldn't?"

"Well," Cindy said, "I didn't know."

"I think we'd *better* have a talk. Could you stay overnight with me? Like tomorrow?"

"It'd have to be Wednesday," Cindy said. "I work at the hospital after school. That means doing homework later. Could I let you know in history class tomorrow?"

Kathy found her mother in the kitchen. "Aren't you finished unpacking *yet?*"

"Oh, yes. Now I'm making out a grocery list, while the list of what we used and brought back is fresh in my mind."

"We didn't bring much back, did we?"

"No, and that's why I'll need to go shopping."

"Makes you think about the pioneers and what they did for food," Kathy said as she filled a glass with water. "They didn't have most of the things we ate. Not even milk unless they had a cow with them. Maybe I wouldn't have liked traveling in a covered wagon after all."

"Some parts you would have probably. Did you get bored while we were away?"

"Not really. I don't understand why. Not for sure."

"What did Cindy have to say that you want to share?"

"Oh, she missed me and went to ask Granddad where we were. Say! I almost forgot! Is it okay if she stays overnight Wednesday?"

"Certainly. It'll be good to have her. It always is."

Kathy stopped in the doorway but didn't turn to face her mother. "You don't say that when Pat and Val come anymore. Not like you did when they first came here."

"I suppose that's true," Lois Miller said. "It's hard for me to say why I've changed—hard to put my inner feelings into words." Then she walked to Kathy and

35

gently turned her so they were face-to-face. "I feel I must say this much. You change when Valerie Harper or Pat is here. You don't with Lucinda."

Kathy's eyes were warm and wet with tears. She hid her face against her mother's shoulder. "Oh, Mom. That makes me sad."

"Me too."

"There's something more you're not saying. I can tell," Kathy said as she blotted tears with a blue tissue. "Something you don't like about my new friends."

"I suppose there is. But I can't tell you what. I can't seem to put it into words. Not yet. Now, you'd better end this day—and so should I. Good-night, dear."

"Good-night, Mom."

It's good to be in a real bed again, Kathy thought as she pulled the lavender blanket up to her chin. *But I sort of dread going to school tomorrow. What will Pat and Val say about me being on what they call "a family drag"—if they say anything at all.*

She kept herself awake until after the clock in the downstairs hall struck ten-thirty. *Why did I think it was so great when Pat and Val paid attention to me? I didn't even know they belonged to the "In Group" then. I'm not even sure I knew there was such a bunch. If we had one at junior high I didn't know it.*

She remembered the first day Val had talked to her. *She was—and I suppose she still is—about the most beautiful girl I've ever seen. Her hair's like clover honey when the sun shines through the jar. And her clothes—white boots up to her knees—and velveteen jumpers. At least that's how she dressed then. Now it's the opposite—patched jeans and sloppy cable knit sweaters. And that beautiful hair's in a shag cut. And*

*every girl in that group looks the same—except me.
And Mom won't let me dress sloppy.*

She went to sleep wondering if she really wanted to copy Val and Pat. And the next morning on the way to school she wished she had enough courage not to go up to them at the water fountain where the group met. *And most of all I wish I didn't care what they say about me. Not so much anyway.*

Pat was at the water fountain but not with Val. It was Wendy Larrimore in the center of the group this time. *Whatever she's saying sure has her excited,* Kathy thought. *She's either waving her hand or shaking a fist all the time.*

Kathy started past the cluster of students but Pat called, "Wait up, Miller! Give us all a chance to cry over you."

"Cry over me?"

"Poor baby," Pat said, "cooped up with family for ages and ages. You're probably in shock—or worse."

"Sorry to disappoint you," Kathy said. "But you're wrong. See you."

"Oh, don't go off mad," Pat said. "We'll take you in."

"Don't bother—"

"Let her go," Wendy Larrimore said. "Who wants a straight messing us up?"

Kathy hurried up the ramp to the second floor. *I'm plain angry,* she thought. She was a little surprised that she didn't feel like crying. *Why? Would I if Val had been in the group? Could be.*

As she turned the knob on the padlock to her locker she heard Val's voice. "I need to talk to you, Kath," she said, "but I have to go to the dean's office. Meet me at noon?"

"Sure," Kathy said. "Why are you going to the dean's office?"

"It's a long story—and a dull one. Deep down dull. Tell you more later. Save a chair at our spot."

I wonder if she's in trouble, Kathy thought as she walked to her first class. *If she ever has been I've not heard about it. She's not that much like Wendy, bold and daring—at least I don't think she is.*

"Where you been?" the boy in the next chair asked as Kathy opened her notebook. "Playing hooky again?"

Kathy smiled. Bill Grayson knew she'd not skip school. "I didn't know where I was for a day and a night."

"What happened? Someone kidnap you—and hold you for ransom?"

"No. And I wasn't blindfolded or drugged. I was stuck in the snow. All of us—my family I mean. In a camper."

"Man! That's tough! I'd like that. Didn't you?"

"Well, as I told Cindy I'm surprised that I wasn't bored or anything."

"What'd you do?"

"I read and took walks and played games with my brother. And fed the birds in the woods."

"Tough!"

As the teacher put the assignment on the board Kathy began to feel calm. *What Wendy and Pat said doesn't seem so upsetting. But I still wonder if Val's in trouble.*

"Where have you been?" Bill asked as Kathy opened her notebook. "Playing hooky again?"

She had carried her tray to the corner table and was setting the bowl of vegetable soup, tossed salad, and butterscotch brownies on the table when Valerie came to the other side. She slammed her shoulder bag down and some of Kathy's soup slurped over the edge of the bowl.

"Who does that monster think she is, blaming us?" Val said in a mean voice. "Just because that square couldn't take it."

"Where's your lunch?" Kathy asked.

"Who can eat after what I've gone through. Have you seen Pat?"

"Not since morning."

"Then I'm going to find her," Val said. "I've got to tell her what happened so her story and mine hang together when she gets called in."

"What story" Kathy began. But she didn't go on. *I'm not sure I want to hear. Besides, Val's gone.*

As she carried her tray to the conveyor belt she tried to find some meaning in what Val had said. *The dean's the monster. That's easy to figure out. But who's the square? What couldn't she take?*

Chapter 5

Cindy was late for history class. *I don't remember that this ever happened before,* Kathy thought as Miss Enright closed the door and walked to her desk. *Surely she's not in whatever trouble there is around here.*

The teacher said, "Review Chapters 23 and 24 in preparation for Friday's test." Several people groaned just as Cindy hurried in and handed an excuse slip to Miss Enright. After she looked at it Kathy heard her ask, "Is Carla any better?"

"Does she mean Carla Trask, Val's cousin who went

41

to school here for a while? That's the only Carla I know.

Kathy waited for Cindy outside the classroom door. "I can stay with you Wednesday night if it's still okay."

"It's great. I got a little worried when you were late—like maybe there's some kind of trouble."

"Well, there is, but not for me—not really. It's about a girl in the hospital. I called her between classes. She needs a friend—really *needs* one. But I have to go now. See you after school tomorrow."

"Where can I meet you?" Kathy asked.

"Anywhere except at the fountain in the front hall. The way I feel now I don't want to go near that place—or that group."

"How about right here? We're both on this floor last period."

"Good. I'll see you then—and at class before."

She was really upset, Kathy thought as she went to the study hall.

At the end of classes she left the building by a side door. As she bypassed the fountain meeting place she saw that Val was not in the group. *And I don't think Pat was. Only Wendy and a few of the others,* she thought as she hurried down the walk. She waited at the curb while the yellow buses pulled out of the parking lot. She waved at two girls who lived out in the township. *I don't know them very well—just from gym class. None of them are in the group. Is it because they have to leave, catch a bus? Or are only town kids included?*

The air was clear and silvered by spring sunshine. *It's hard to believe we were in a storm two days ago.*

42

Almost all the snow is melted. Except in splotches on the yard. They make the grass look like a giant spice cookie—like the ones Grandmother Miller keeps in the yellow jar. The white icing is sort of splashed on.

Will Val call me tonight? she thought as she unlatched the back gate. *I'd like to know why she had to go to the dean's office. It'd be nosy of me to call her, but I can't help being curious—about lots of things.*

Clothes were flipping and flapping on the wire line. "Is the dryer broken?" she asked as she walked into the kitchen.

"No. But I like the way clothes smell when they're air dried. And this is the kind of day for that, breezy and sunny. Do you suppose I have a touch of the pioneer spirit—because of having been snowbound?"

"Looks like it! You've even baked bread. I wondered what smelled so *delish*."

"You know me," her mother said. "I do things by spells."

"Anyone call?"

"Give them time. And in the meanwhile help yourself to some bread. Don't bear down with the knife or you'll squash it."

As Kathy spread grape jelly on the warm bread she said, "Cindy's coming Wednesday night."

"Good. As it worked out that's better than having her tonight. Of course she'd be welcome to go with us."

"Go? Go where?" Kathy asked.

"Out to Oakville. Your grandfather came to town, he said, to invite us out for supper. But your father thinks there's another reason—business of some kind. He thinks that has something to do with why we're invited."

"Good or bad?"

"I'd say good—from what I heard—which wasn't much."

"I'm glad," Kathy said. "A lot of bad vibes were going on at school."

"Vibes—oh, you mean vibrations. I'd like to hear what you care to tell. But I see you have homework."

"Yes. A lot—because of needing to catch up. Besides, I don't *know* much."

Kathy was reviewing her history notes when Wayne came to her door. She'd left this assignment till last because the test wouldn't be given until Friday. "Mom says we're ready to go. And don't poke."

"Who's poking? I sure hope Grandma has chicken and dumplings."

"Doesn't she always when we're there?"

Kathy and her brother reached the car as their parents came out the back door. "Hi, Skip," Wayne said as he waved to a boy on a bicycle.

"Who was that?"

"A guy in my class. Skip Trask."

"You know him?"

"Sure. How else would I know his name?"

"I wonder if he's related to the girl who went here—Carla Trask?"

"She's his sister—the one in the hospital," Wayne said.

"What's wrong?"

"I don't know. Skip doesn't talk about it except to say he hope she gets home."

As they rode toward Oakville Kathy tried to remember what she'd heard about Carla. *Did anyone tell me she'd moved? Or did I just think so because she*

44

wasn't around? I'm for sure going to ask Cindy about this.

Kathy was ladling creamy dumplings on to her plate when her grandfather told them what was on his mind.

"No use beating around the bush. I'd like to have a part-time job in your store," Mr. Miller said.

"You're hired," Rex Miller said. "But why? To help me over a rough spot?"

"Partly."

"Or to smooth over what Ken did, leaving the business all of a sudden?" Lois Miller asked.

"Partly."

"He's not telling you the whole truth," Kathy's grandmother said. "He's bored after only five months of retirement. He doesn't know what to do with himself."

"And you're getting tired of having me underfoot. Own up, Mother."

"Only if you're unhappy, John. You know that."

Mr. Miller went on talking as they ate. He said that he'd felt alive while he was minding the store. "I've missed talking to people more than I realized." He said he'd gone to look at pickup trucks so that Rex's mother could have the car to use.

"You know how much you want to work, Dad?"

"Well, I figured I could do you the most good on Tuesday and Friday, when new stock comes in. And how would it be to relieve each other on Saturdays— when either of us wants to go away?"

"Except that Saturdays are often busy days, aren't they?" Lois Miller asked.

"True," Rex Miller said. "But I think a way will work out. In fact, I'm sure it will."

45

"How can you be *sure?*" Kathy asked.

"I can't answer you. I guess I'm doing some positive thinking for a change. That's what your granddad's helping hand has done for me already."

"Is school going all right for you this year, Kathryn?" Mrs. Miller asked as they carried dishes to the kitchen.

"Mostly, Grandma."

"You aren't having problems, are you? You've always done so well."

"I'm not having problems with classes or teachers. But, well, sometimes I think friendship—what it means—is different."

"We've talked about this before. Remember?"

"I know. Back when someone wouldn't play with me—or called me bossy or something."

"Are girls not *playing* with you now—or calling you names? Or should I ask?"

"It's a lot the same I guess. Some let you in the group—if you go by their rules. And the names! Grandma, I could never repeat some of the things they say—not to anyone."

"Isn't there anyone else who feels as you do?"

"Probably. Well, I do know *one.* Cindy Masters. She's staying all night with me tomorrow. We used to be together a lot at the other school."

Kathy's parents talked all the way home. She could tell they felt better about things, that they were relieved to know there'd be someone to help in the building supply store. As they stopped outside the garage Lois Miller turned to ask, "Are you two asleep?"

"I'm not," Kathy said.

"Me neither," Wayne answered.

"You haven't said a word all the way from Oakville."

"I'm too full of dumplings," Wayne said.

"And I was listening to you and Dad. You sounded happier than you have for along time. I'm glad."

Chapter 6

The next morning Kathy was ready to cross the street which ran in front of the school when a car horn blared and tires screeched. *Why is that driver so steamed up? I'm on the curb.* The low orange sports car passed her and turned into the school lot with more tire squealing. *Why, that's Wendy. I've seen her with that boy before. He must be from the other high school.*

Wendy waited at the triple set of doors which surprised Kathy. *She never pays attention to me unless we're in the group—and not much then.*

48

"You hear about Harper?" Wendy asked.

"No, unless you mean about being called to the dean's office."

"That's what I mean! And the what for. When I think of how that—"

"Don't, Wendy."

"Don't what?"

"Don't use that kind of language—not to me."

"Well!" Wendy said. "So! I was right all the time. I laid it on Pat and Val—really heavy. I said you'd be *another* ratting squealer."

Kathy felt her cheeks getting hot. She turned and walked in the opposite direction. *It'll mean going up the east ramp and doubling back, but that's okay.*

She avoided going near the fountain meeting place all day and was relieved in a way that neither Pat nor Valerie were in her classes. She went to the library during study hall periods and didn't see anyone who might know what kind of trouble was going on until the next to last class when she saw Cindy.

"Did you see the notice on the bulletin board—about forming a student council?"

"No. I didn't stop there coming in. How they going about it?"

"It didn't say—just that steps were being taken."

The girls walked out of the building and into a spring rain shower. "That came up in a hurry," Kathy said. "The sun was out when we left history class. We'd better step back inside until it lets up a little. In seven blocks we'd be soaking wet."

"Did you hear someone calling you?" Cindy asked.

"No—oh, sure! There's my mother out in the lot. Let's make a dash for the car."

"You'd better squeeze in the front," Lois Miller said as she opened the door. "The back's full of wall tile."

"For where?" Kathy asked.

"For the church—the nursery classroom. I'll deliver it after I taxi you girls home."

"Why not let us go with you?" Cindy asked. "We'll help you unload those boxes."

"That's an offer I'll not refuse. It shouldn't take long—with three pairs of hands."

Kathy heard the sound of music as she bumped her shoulder against the swinging door of the church basement. "Someone's practicing on the organ."

"I heard," Cindy said. "That's 'Amazing Grace.' It makes me feel so good inside. I'm trying to learn it."

"Are you taking lessons on the organ?"

"On the piano."

"I didn't know that. When do you have time?"

"Oh, I guess we manage to do what seems most important."

"I suppose," Kathy said. "If we know—or take time to find out."

The April shower had stopped by the time the cartons were stored in the church basement. "Everything looks so fresh and alive," Kathy's mother said. "I even saw some furry pussy willow buds as I crossed the yard this morning."

"You didn't bring much homework either," Kathy said as she and Cindy went upstairs toward her room.

"Just history. I thought we could review together."

"That's what I thought. Are you hungry? I should have asked before we came upstairs."

"Your mother did already—while you went back to the car for your book. I said I'd rather wait for whatever smelled so good."

"Lasagna, for one thing."

Kathy felt a little uneasy and she wasn't sure why. *It's not like Cindy and I ever had a fight. And I feel the same about her. Maybe I'm scared she's changed— toward me.*

"Play records if you like," Kathy said. "I have some new ones since you've been here." Then she sat down on the end of one bed so hard that the pillow on the other end made a little bounce. "Cindy, I have to say this—just have to! I don't know where my head was, thinking it was so great being with the 'In Group.' "

"You saying it's not?"

"I sure am! I mean—well, there are some bad vibes."

"There always have been for me—and more now since I've known about Carla."

"You mean there's a connection—between people in the 'In Group' and Carla Trask?"

"Yes, and between them and what happened to her. You don't know about that?"

"No. I thought she'd moved."

"No. She's had an emotional illness, a kind of break-down," Cindy said. "But I don't think I'd better say what caused it. She asked me not to tell."

"Then you shouldn't," Kathy said. "But I wish I understood. Anyway, I'm dropping out. I've had it! Especially with Pat and Wendy."

"That's what Carla thought—that she could drop out whenever she wanted and that would end things."

"Why not?"

"All I'm going to say is, be careful."

"Well, maybe I'll talk to Val first."

51

"That's what Carla did."

Kathy brushed her hair to the side of her forehead. "You don't like Val either."

"Don't make me say, Kathy. I know how Valerie seems to you—beautiful and friendly—at first. You have to make up your own mind who you choose for a friend."

"You think I chose Val over you, Cindy. But that's not true. I like both of you."

"But things don't always work out like that. I mean I do some things that would bore Val. And well—I couldn't go along with her."

Kathy took a deep breath. "Something's all mixed up. Me, maybe."

"Let's change the subject. Okay?"

"Sure. How about a bike ride? Dad won't be home for an hour."

"I'd like that."

"One of us will have to ride Wayne's."

"I will," Cindy said. "My legs are longer and my skirt is pleated."

They rode in the opposite direction from the high school. There was less traffic and most of the time they stayed on the street. When they came to Woodbridge Elementary School Cindy called, "I see Mrs. Allen's car. She always stays late."

"I haven't seen her for a long time," Kathy said as she put a foot to the pavement and came to a stop.

"I come past sometimes," Cindy said. "Especially since Mr. Allen died."

"I didn't even know he had."

"Last fall—soon after school started."

"I wonder if we could get in now to see her."

Probably not. They lock the door at four—because some kids tear things up. I always call and Mrs. A. lets me in."

"I'll do that some day soon. Anyway, it's probably about time to eat—or it will be by the time we get back."

Kathy felt comfortable the rest of the evening. The girls washed and put away the dishes while Lois Miller melted marshmallows over Rice Krispies. The five who were together for the first time in many months had much to share. Cindy wanted to hear more about the experience of being snowbound and kept saying, "I'd have loved *that*." She told the Millers about some of the people she'd met at the hospital and that her mother was taking night classes at the Career Center. "Ask her to bake a cake for you and do *us* a favor, Mrs. Miller," Cindy teased. "She's taking decorating now and is practicing on us. Enough's enough of anything, even cake!"

The telephone rang as they went to the sun porch to watch a special on television.

"It's for you, Kathy," Wayne said.

When Val answered, Kathy looked toward Cindy and frowned. "I can't talk now, Valerie, I'm busy."

"Busy! Doing what?"

"I have company."

"Then call me back."

"Not tonight, Val."

"Well, if that's the way you feel"

"It is. Good-bye."

I'm amazed at myself, she thought as she followed the others. *I've never, never made Val wait—never put her off. I've never had the nerve.*

Before they went to bed Cindy and Kathy quizzed each other on the review chapters and ate marshmallow squares. Then they listened to both sides of a stack of records, talking only now and then. They'd turned out the light and been quiet for several minutes when Cindy said. "It's good."

"Good?"

"Good to pick up where you left off with someone."

"I know what you mean," Kathy said. She turned her head and looked out the window. She couldn't see much except the darkened sky and the tips of the Lombardy poplar tree at the corner of the front yard. It was warm enough to have the window up a few inches. The chimes in the church tower began to mark the hour of ten. "But I can't help wishing something."

"Such as what?"

"That we hadn't left off—or that I hadn't."

Kathy knew she should let herself drift into sleep. *But I've got to get something straightened out first,* she thought. *Or try.* She could see now that Val wasn't the kind of person she'd thought. And hearing that Carla Trask's illness was in some way connected to Val and the "In Group" was proof. *But why didn't I see that as clearly as Cindy did?*

For some reason she thought of her long-time favorite book about life in a covered wagon. *On our camping trip I saw that living that way wasn't as great as I had imagined. I guess I was too impressed with Val's clothes and that she was pretty and popular and*

"I know teenagers well enough to realize that you're not all alike," Kathy's mother told her.

overlooked what kind of a person she is inside.

Somehow I feel better, Kathy thought as she turned toward the wall. *Like I'm understanding more—even myself.*

She was asleep, or nearly so, when her mother came to her bed. "Kathy, can you slip out in the hall?" she whispered. "I don't want to wake Cindy."

Kathy stumbled over her fuzzy slippers as she caught up with her mother. "What's wrong?"

"Nothing. Not with any of us. Who was that on the phone earlier?"

"Val. Why?"

"Well Mrs. Harper called me out of bed. She wants to know if Valerie is here."

"Is she still on the phone?"

"Yes, she's waiting."

"I don't know where she is. I supposed she was home when she called me."

"You don't want to talk to Mrs. Harper?"

"No, Mom. I don't know anything—except that Val was called into the dean's office. And I don't want to tell her *that*."

"No. That's not for us to say."

Kathy sat down on the top step until her mother finished talking to Mrs. Harper.

"What'd she say? Was she upset?"

"Not really. Not as much as I'd be. She just laughed and said, 'She'll turn up. When she's ready. You know teenagers.'"

"Do you, Mom? Do you know teenagers?"

Lois Miller stopped, cupped Kathy's face in her hands, and said, "Well enough to realize that you're not all alike—for which I'm grateful."

Chapter 7

Kathy's father was on the telephone when the girls started downstairs the next morning. He smiled and touched a finger to his lips. When he came to the breakfast table he asked, "How do you people like the idea of taking a train trip—to Chicago?"

"Neat!" Wayne said. "Great. When?"

"Wayne," Kathy said, "no one says 'neat' anymore."

"I do," her brother said, "And I'm someone."

"Why?" Lois Miller asked. "Why go to Chicago?"

"There's a home show a couple of weeks from now—where the emphasis is on remodeling. We have a lot of that kind of business."

"I'd like it, Dad," Kathy said.

"How about you, Cindy?" Rex Miller asked. "Do you think your parents would let you go?"

"You don't have to include me, Mr. Miller, just because I'm here," Cindy said.

"Oh, Cindy, please," Kathy said. "I'd like it if you went."

"That goes for all of us," Lois Miller said. "You know something? I've thought every once in awhile that we ought to go someplace on the train, now that Amtrak's been rerouted through Muncie and we can get on and off right here."

"You ask your parents, Cindy," Kathy's father said. "I'm fairly sure that Dad will take over for me. We'd leave early on Friday."

"You mean we'd skip school?" Wayne asked.

"Not skip," his mother said. "Get excused."

The girls talked about the idea of going on the train as they walked to school. They were so involved in plans that they didn't realize they were walking toward the meeting place of the "In Group" until Wendy Larrimore said, "Well! See for yourself, all of you. Birds of a feather do flock together—squawking-type birds."

Kathy wanted to hurry on to the ramp, but stopped when she saw that Cindy was walking toward Wendy. *What's she going to do? I can't run out on her—even if I'd rather—a whole lot rather.*

At first Cindy didn't say anything. She stood and looked straight at Wendy. Then she began to talk. Her voice was soft, even gentle. *It's surprising that we can hear her, with people coming in the door all the time,* Kathy thought.

"I know I'll be spoiling your fun," Cindy said. "But you're not hurting me. You can't do that to me anymore—not after I learned how you've damaged others by your ridicule and making fun of what they thought was good."

Does she mean Carla Trask? Kathy wondered. *Or are there others?*

"You can't hurt anyone like that," Cindy went on, "unless they think your opinion is all that important. You see, I *don't.*"

No one in the "In Group" said a word, at least not while Cindy and Kathy were within hearing distance. One or two had looked down as Cindy talked and Pat had taken a couple of steps back from Wendy. Kathy had watched Val's face most of the time and saw a line of white around her mouth. *She's furious.*

Kathy drew a deep breath as they stepped off the ramp into the second floor hall. "Weren't you scared?"

"No. Not really," Cindy said. "But not because I'm all that *brave.*"

"Why then?"

"Because—because of more than one thing. You see, I've rehearsed what I'd say to that group if I ever did get up the nerve to face them."

"Did it come out like you meant?"

"As I meant, yes, but not the same words probably. To tell the truth, I really couldn't tell you what I said, not right now."

"I can tell you—or I could if the bell wasn't ringing."

As she went on to her first period class Kathy realized Cindy hadn't mentioned the other reason, or reasons, she hadn't been afraid to come face-to-face with Wendy and the others. *I'll ask her later.*

Neither Val nor Pat spoke to Kathy when they met in the hall or the classrooms or the cafeteria. She felt uncomfortable about being shunned until it came to her that she'd feel worse if they said what they were thinking. She'd taken her tray to the usual table at noon, then decided to move when she saw the members of the "In Group" in line together. As she sprinkled salt over her succotash she counted the people in the line. *There are fourteen. I've never even thought of how many were included. Were there only fifteen—with me? Not very many really. Not enough to make them feel so important—not in numbers anyway.*

She left the cafeteria and started toward the library, but stopped when she saw the red-framed notice on the bulletin board. Notices from the office were always posted on red construction paper. She shifted her books to keep them from slipping and read, "These people are asked to meet at the dean's office at 3:00 p.m. on Friday. The purpose of the meeting is to discuss the idea of a student council."

Cindy will be on there, I'm sure, Kathy thought. She knew most of the people whose names were listed. *Bill Grayson and one of those Oakville girls—the one named Jill. And—me. Why me?*

Kathy was frightened. "Is Valerie taking me to the other 'In Group' members?" she wondered.

60

Before sixth period class could begin the principal's voice came over the intercom system. *This must be something important,* Kathy thought. *Usually the dean or assistant principal makes during-the-day announcements.*

"It has become necessary for us to make a new ruling to become effective immediately," Mr. Jordan said. "The halls will no longer be used for meeting places for groups. We hope that we will not need to position teachers to enforce this decision, but we will if there are violations. Unfortunately certain individuals have abused the freedom to congregate."

Kathy glanced sideways at Pat without turning her head. *She has to know this rule was made because of the "In Group." At least that's how it seems to me.*

"What are you going—" Kathy started to ask when she met Cindy on the way to history class. "Oh, I forgot you go to the hospital tonight."

"Yes."

There was time for Kathy to ask, "Were you surprised when Mr. Jordan made that announcement?"

"Surprised? Maybe a little. Relieved is the best word to describe how I felt."

Kathy meant to leave school by the side door, but remembered that she needed a book from the library. *If I hurry Mrs. Lambert will still be there.* As she left with the book she saw Valerie Harper leaning against the wall. *Is she waiting for me?*

"You can't run from me," Valerie said as she stepped to meet Kathy. "And you don't have your body guard."

"We're not supposed to congregate."

"Who's congregating? Keep walking."

62

Kathy was frightened. She could feel the pulsing of her heart in her throat. *Is she taking me to the other "In Group" members? Surely they wouldn't actually hurt me, would they?*

"I've got a lot of things to say to you, Miller! Not all at once. But don't forget this! The group's not done for—and not done with you. No one—no one ever snitches on us without wishing they had kept their big mouth shut."

"Oh, Val. Don't be so—so dramatic. You sound like an old gangster movie. And what could I snitch—as you put it?"

"Don't pull that innocent act on me. Now I see through you. Why did I bother to put pressure on the others to let you in? That's what I'd like to know."

"Let me in?" Kathy said. "I didn't know anyone was let in. I thought we just sort of drifted together."

"Not so! You don't think we want everyone to hear stuff."

"I don't want to talk to you any longer, Val. And I wish I hadn't heard a lot of the group's klunky talk."

"Do you think we'd have let you hear if we hadn't thought you wanted in? We thought you wouldn't blab. We made a mistake with Carla. And to think she's my cousin. What she got she deserves."

They were outside the building and Kathy stopped at the end of the walk and faced Valerie. "I thought I knew you! How could a person be so wrong? You're hard and cruel. Really hard."

"Now you know! And don't forget it."

Kathy almost ran across the street. She couldn't wait until she got home. She remembered how she felt the night they were snowbound in the camper. *The only word that comes into my mind is shelter. Isn't that about the same as safe?*

She felt let down when Wayne met her at the back door. "Mom's not here," he said. "There's a note. We can go too."

"Go where?"

"To Mrs. Wardelle's to help her move some flowers. Mom said so on the note."

"You going?"

"Sure. Mrs. Wardelle makes great doughnuts. How about you?"

"I think I'll stay here."

"Okay. See you later."

In a way Kathy was relieved that her mother was not at home and that she could be alone for a while. *I'd probably blurt out everything that happened at school. And it might not make much sense to Mom. How could it? I don't understand—yes, I do—some anyway. I know what Val doesn't want me to tell. The stuff the girls told each other about being out with boys. But I never really listened. I either walked away or thought the girls were stretching things—to impress each other. Besides, I couldn't say things like that to Mom.*

She walked from window to window but really didn't see much. *Everything's so mixed up*, she thought. *Will school and friendship ever seem good to me again?* She saw Wayne's bike leaning against the garage and that led her to remember the ride she'd taken with Cindy. *I wish I could talk to Mrs. Allen. I don't know what I'd say—not now—only that it seems like a good idea.*

She hurried to the telephone but no one answered at

Woodbridge School. *They're probably all gone already. I guess Val kept me longer than I realized. I think I'll take a ride by myself—after I go past and ask Mom if it's okay."*

As she kicked the bike stand to the catch she thought of something Pat had said to her a few times. "You can't mean that you do what your parents say?"

"Most of the time," Kathy had answered. "Well, always, really. Don't you?"

"Oh, I ask—to throw them off my track. But that's the end! And you can believe this. Asking relieves them too. It takes a load off them. They don't care what I do—just so I go through the motions."

It's not like that at our house, Kathy wanted to say. *But I didn't,* she thought as she rode around the corner. *A lot of times I kept quiet. Because I didn't want them to think I was a drag. It seems cowardly now—or worse, maybe even dishonest.*

After promising her mother she'd start home when the chimes in the church tower let her know it was four-thirty, Kathy rode west on Godman Avenue. She bumped over the railroad tracks and went beyond the jog in the street. She rode fast after the traffic thinned and liked the feel of the wind against her face. The thought of the trouble at school seemed to be erased from her mind as she moved. She was away from all that—for awhile.

Chapter 8

Cindy called before Kathy finished her home work. "I just now got home from the hospital and have great news. Carla gets to go home the last of next week. The doctor says she can begin doing makeup work then and I was wondering, would you have time to help her? Could you get the back assignments from her teachers and sort of give her a lift?"

"Yes, I'd like to help," Kathy said. But she didn't express another thought. *Will I have to be careful what I say about school?*

"She knows about the rule Mr. Jordan made today," Cindy said.

"You talked to her about Val and the others?"

"Oh, yes. And I think she'll do that with you, after awhile."

"Well, I don't see how she could feel right about mentioning the 'In Group' to me. She knows I hung around with them. She knows you're not like them."

"How could she?"

"Well, for one thing—I told her. I'd better get to my homework. You probably have yours done already."

"Not quite. Is it okay if I call you back after I ask Mom if I can help Carla—and after I see if there are any questions I can't answer?"

"Sure. But I may not have all the answers."

"Who does?"

Kathy went downstairs and chatted with her family for a few minutes after she'd finished her assignments. *I'll give Cindy time to do hers before I call back.* When her mother said she'd forgotten to take a roast out of the freezer, Kathy followed her to the kitchen. She told her about the idea of helping Carla. "She's a girl who's in the hospital with some kind of a breakdown."

"It sounds like a good thing. Do you want to do it?"

"Yes, I do," Kathy said. "But in another way I dread it. I've never been around anyone who had emotional problems."

"I'd say you probably have and didn't know it," Lois Miller said. "Many people have anxieties and fears and cover them up when they're around others— or try to. Just be kind to Carla if you do decide to help her."

"I've decided. I just don't want to do the wrong thing."

"By the way, I didn't ask you. How was school?"

"Oh—okay—No, it wasn't at all! Could we go somewhere and talk?"

"What's wrong with here? Pull out a chair. I'll get us some fruit punch."

"You know what I told you before—about the girls, Val and Pat, putting me down because I'm embarrassed by the way they talk?"

"I remember."

"Well, Mom, it's a lot worse than I let on—maybe worse than I even know." She went on to tell that the "In Group" girls met at the water fountain every morning. And that many times, especially on Mondays they talked mostly about their dates—what they did on them."

"And you listened?"

"Sometimes. But I thought they were bragging or making things up."

"Well—you know how I feel about the dating—at your age."

"I know. And I don't want to—not now—not after what I heard. It's scary. And I wouldn't ever invent stuff like that just to keep up."

Lois Miller reached across the table and cupped Kathy's doubled up fist in one hand. "I have to ask this, dear. Why did you think it was so important to be included in that group?"

"It's not easy to understand now. I'm not proud of myself about the whole thing. I'm ashamed really."

"How much did Valerie's influence have to do with it?"

"A lot, I guess. She's so lovely. At least I thought she was. And I felt flattered when she began to ask me to eat at the table with her and to meet at the fountain. But Mom, she's cruel."

"To you?"

"Today she was. You see, there's trouble," Kathy said. She went on to tell what she knew about Carla's illness. "Cindy can't tell me but I know that the 'In Group' is to blame somehow." She told how Mr. Jordan had announced that groups shouldn't congregate in the halls and that Val had in a way threatened her after school.

"Why?" Kathy's mother said. "What could you do to hurt her? Or what would you do?"

"I don't know, unless she thinks I might repeat some of the things she *says* she does."

"But if she brags, as you say, why would she care if anyone else talked about it."

"I don't know, unless she doesn't want her parents or the teachers to know."

"Do you think you've learned anything from this experience?" Kathy's mother asked. "Here let me fill your glass."

"I hope so," Kathy said. "Things haven't been much fun lately."

She left the kitchen and walked to the front door. The street was empty and no one was on the sidewalk except the Conroy twins. She watched as the little girls rode their tricycles down toward the corner. *They aren't racing—only riding.*

She went outside and sat on the top step of the three layers of flagstone. "Hi, Kathy," Dina said.

"Hi, yourself. Who's your friend?"

"You know who I am. I'm Doris."

"Right! I thought you looked like someone I'd seen."

"I know why you speak to only one of us at a time," Dina said.

"You do, do you?"

"Yes. 'Cause you can't tell us apart. And the one who answers tells you who the other is."

"Well, you found me out," Kathy said.

"Don't feel bad. About everybody does that. Except Mama and Daddy sometimes. And Mrs. Allen."

"Is she your teacher?"

"She's mine," Doris said. "They don't put twins in the same room. But Mrs. Allen knows us from each other when we're together."

"So do I when you're close like now," Kathy said. "When I can see Dina's dimple."

The seven-year-olds sat down, one on either side of Kathy. They watched a kite dip and rise against the evening sky. "You can't see the string, but I know it's there," Doris said.

"How?"

" 'Cause it'd go up and up and up without one— and never come down, ever."

Kathy remembered when she was five and her father had gone to a vacant lot to fly the red and green kite he'd brought home. It had seemed funny to see her father running so the movement would make some more breeze. He'd said, "When it gets above the trees you can hold the string." Then the breeze died down, the kite dipped, caught a limb and the string snapped. The triangle of paper and balsa wood was soon out of sight. "I'm sorry, honey," Kathy's father said. "I'll get you another."

70

"Don't feel bad, Dad," Kathy had said. "God probably needed a kite."

That time seems so far away, Kathy thought. *And so good.* "Say, you two. How'd you like for me to take you for a ride on my bike? You could take turns."

"Yes, yes," the twins said.

"Better ask your Mama. Tell her we'll only go around the block."

After each girl had taken two rides Kathy said, "It'll soon be dark now. We'd better go."

"Thank you for the ride," Dina said.

"Me too," Doris added. "I'm glad you're not all the way grown up, Kathy."

"So am I!"

Kathy blinked as she walked into the light of the kitchen and followed the sound of her mother's voice to the telephone. "That for me?" she whispered. When her mother shook her head she started up to her room.

"That was Mrs. Allen," Kathy's mother said as she put the telephone on its cradle. "But Cindy called earlier. She said she'd talk to you tomorrow. Her family decided to visit someone—a cousin, I think she said."

"I was supposed to tell her it's okay with you if I help Carla."

"I told her. What are you going to do with yourself this evening?"

"I don't know. Read maybe and listen to records. Why?"

"Oh, I thought about taking a walk to see Mrs. Allen. When I talked to her awhile ago she sounded lonely. Want to go?"

71

"Sure. Wait until I get a sweater. It's getting chilly."

As they crossed the street and went down Calvert Avenue Kathy said, "It's funny how Mrs. Allen's name keeps coming up. Cindy was talking about her and tonight the Conroy girls mentioned her name. Now you."

"That's not strange, really. She's a wonderful person and has touched the lives of many of us for good."

I wonder if Val was ever in Mrs. Allen's room? Kathy thought. *She isn't showing many signs of a good influence. But I guess Mrs. Allen can't be held responsible for everyone.*

"I should have thought to bring some pussy willows."

"I can run back."

"Would you?"

"Sure. I remember I took some for Mrs. Allen's room for as long as I went to Woodbridge."

As Kathy bent the fuzzy tufted branches she remembered the pink and gray vase in which the teacher placed the pussy willows. She said her son sent it to her when he was overseas in Germany. *I wonder where he is now?*

"Do you know anything about Mrs. Allen's son?" Kathy asked, as she caught up with her mother.

"What made you think of him? You can't remember him."

"No. But she talked about him and the things he brought back from Germany."

"*Sent* back. He never came home. He was due to leave when he was killed in an accident."

"That's sad. I remember how Mrs. Allen looked

when she mentioned his name—so loving and proud."

"I know. That was a blow and I don't think the Allens ever recovered. They stayed to themselves more. Oh they went on working, but they didn't go out much."

"No wonder she's lonely."

"True. I'm afraid we've not been Good Samaritans. We've ignored her needs."

"I haven't heard anyone talk about being a Good Samaritan for a long time, except in Sunday school once in awhile."

"Probably because we don't think about it as much as we should. If we did we'd talk more often about being helpful and probably we'd be more helpful.

Mrs. Allen met them at the door. *She looks the same—maybe a little sadder,* Kathy thought.

"Oh, pussy willows! You remember how I love them. Thank you. I'm so glad you came along, Kathryn. And I'm not going to say, 'How you've grown.' That's to be expected, isn't it?"

"Your room is lovely," Lois Miller said. "I love the color combination you've used. Pale pink—and is it mauve?"

"Yes, or delicate purple. I haven't used this room much lately. I keep holed up in the kitchen and dining room most of the time. But now it's April and it's getting warmer. I've often said spring's a time of resurrection. But until the last few days I wasn't at all sure I'd ever feel that way again.

Chapter 9

As Kathy listened to the conversation between her mother and the lady who'd been her second-grade teacher she realized that Valerie's ideas were different from hers in another way. *Val always says older people are boring and think they know all there is to know about everything.*

They do, Kathy thought as she listened. *They know a lot more than we do. The difference is I'm not bored. How could Val be if she really listened?*

Kathy's mother had led into the subject they were

on by asking, "Am I right? Is that a real gas lamp over your desk?"

"Yes, it is. Of course it's there for a purely decorative purpose—or is sentimental a better word?" She went on to tell that the house had been built by Mr. Allen's grandfather. "This was the edge of town then and the gas boom was going strong."

I'm hearing history, Kathy thought as Mrs. Allen told about gas wells being located all over the countryside. "The gas burned in the daytime and at night flames flared from pipes."

"Wasn't that wasteful?" Kathy asked.

"It was and that's one reason the natural gas supply in these parts has run out."

The conversation drifted from one subject to another. Talk of changes in the town led the women to recall people they'd both known. "You remember Mr. Merton?" Mrs. Allen asked.

"Certainly. He was principal when I was in Woodbridge," Kathy's mother said.

"And back farther, when I was in elementary school, too. He was still there the first eleven years I taught," Mrs. Allen said. "I think of him often and wonder how he would handle some of the problems we're faced with today."

"Are they much different?" Lois Miller asked.

The room was still for a few minutes. Kathy watched the brass pendulum of the tall clock as it swung—up so far, down—then up as far on the opposite side. "No. They're not—different. At first I was about to say, yes. The causes are the same—unkindness, carelessness, laziness, lack of confidence, and a basketful of other faults and needs. It's the intensity that makes them *seem* different. For example, even when Kathryn was in school cases of child abuse or alcoholism or even broken homes were, if not rare, at least infrequent."

"And these are damaging to a child. Anyone can see that," Lois Miller said.

"Not everyone does! But that's not the worst—or the most difficult to me to handle," Mrs. Allen said. "It's ridicule, belittling, putting people down, making fun of them—whatever you want to call it."

"Hasn't this always gone on?" Kathy was ready to ask when her mother put the same thought into words.

"There's been a change and I don't know when it began. Now, children are the target of taunts because of their strong or good points." She told of one second grader who'd suffered for days because some of the other children called him a red-neck.

"What did they mean?" Lois Miller asked. "Was he sunburned? Did he have a rash?"

"No, Mom," Kathy said. "He has short hair."

"Correct," Mrs. Allen said. "He's neat and clean. His mother wouldn't let him come to school any other way. Now some of the long hair is as well cared for."

"But that's not the point," Mrs. Miller said. "It's the label—the taunting tone that hurts. You talked to him, I'm sure of that."

"Yes. I told him that even if the children said bad things about something good, it was still good. I don't know if I helped or not."

"In that connection," Lois Miller said, "there's a lesson I didn't learn until I was much older than Kathy."

"What, Mom?"

"That in a way it's a compliment when some people

76

ridicule you—if their values and standards are lower than yours."

"That's correct," Mrs. Allen said.

They could be talking about me or to me, Kathy thought.

"My goodness! Look at the clock. We should have left a half hour ago. It's past the Miller's curfew hour."

"It's been cold water to my thirsty soul to have you here." Mrs. Allen said. "You'll come back?"

"We'll come back," Lois Miller promised as she turned and waved. "It's nice to renew good relationships when you can."

"What do you mean when you can?" Kathy asked.

"Well, people change—or is it that they don't sometimes. I see someone now and then that had been a close friend and I always feel sad when we can't think of anything to say except, 'How have you been?' and 'It's been a long time.' "

"That's *not* too interesting a conversation," Kathy said.

"And it doesn't last long either, fortunately!"

Kathy didn't try to call Cindy. *They probably aren't back yet. And Mom told her it's all right if I help Carla Trask. It's not like it was with Val and Pat. We don't have to call each other all the time.*

"You going to watch TV?" Wayne asked as Kathy started toward the sun-room.

"I was planning to—for a while. Why aren't you?"

"Because I can't. I have to learn this long poem."

"How long? The way you sound it could be like a chapter."

"Fifteen lines. That's long enough! More than enough."

"Want me to hold the book?"

"I was wondering if you would."

"I don't see why you're so upset," Kathy said. "You don't have any trouble memorizing."

"It's not remembering a poem that's rough. It's saying it. Kids make faces and do dumb things."

"I know," Kathy said. "Can't you ignore them and look at a picture on the wall or something? I used to look at Cindy."

"I'd rather shut my eyes, but the teacher wouldn't like that."

"Then look at her. She's okay, isn't she?"

"Yes, she's okay. She never puts anybody down."

Is it happening in his room too? she thought as Wayne went to get his book.

With only a few promptings Wayne decided he was ready to perform. "Of course by tomorrow my mind may be blank," he muttered.

"I doubt it," Kathy said. "How'd you like it if I ask Mom if it's too late to make some popcorn?"

"It's too late. My bedtime's in ten minutes. It's not fair that you can stay up half an hour longer."

"Not tonight. I'm going up right behind you."

Kathy was in bed listening to records when her father rapped on the door—three knocks, a pause, then another knock. "Come in. I'm awake."

"That's obvious, unless you're talking in your sleep. I'll not stay long. Your Mother says you're going through a bad time," Rex Miller said as he sat down on the foot of the bed.

"I wish I was all the way through it," Kathy said, "not still going."

"Want to talk about it—to me?"

"I don't *not* want to," Kathy said. "It's just that I'm not too proud of myself about some parts."

"Such as?"

"Such as thinking it was important to be a member of the 'In Group.' I practically fell over myself being where those girls were, especially Val."

"Not having any experience as a girl this may come out sounding stupid, but isn't wanting to be accepted normal?"

"Maybe. But after I was in I couldn't make myself keep believing it was that tough—not all the time."

"Tough?"

"That means great, the best."

"It didn't mean that when I was your age. It meant—tough. I don't believe there'd be such a communication gap if kids didn't keep changing the language."

The evening breeze made the ends of the ruffled curtains blow out into the room. Kathy heard several ticks of her small brass clock before her father spoke. "*And* it might help if we grown-ups were more careful about what *we* say—if we really lived the way we say we believe people should."

"You do, Dad. You're not dishonest with me."

"I don't intend to be. That's something I can't understand. I know men who stand in the store and vow that their sons or daughters will be grounded or whipped if they use drugs or drink or even smoke. It doesn't add up, when I know they smoke and drink, and that alcohol's a drug."

"You're talking about setting an example, aren't you?"

"I am. I guess we do all the time—either good or

bad. But going back to the way you're feeling. Don't whip yourself too hard, honey. You didn't know what you were getting into."

Kathy wiped her eyes with the tail of her pajama top. "No, I didn't. After I was with them a lot, I knew. The girls were different when they were all together— at least not like I thought."

"It's time I let you get to sleep. Good-night."

"Good-night, Daddy. Thank you for coming in."

After her father left, Kathy turned over and rested her head on one doubled arm. *I wonder about Val. I don't know much about her mother and nothing about her father except that he lives in Kansas or someplace far from here.*

Are they bad examples? She tried to remember what she'd heard about the families of the other girls. *Not much really. Surely some of them come from homes where they're loved. Everything that's happened couldn't be blamed on parents.*

She felt thirsty and was wide awake by the time she tiptoed back from the bathroom. *I think I'll read to try to erase all these worries.*

The next morning she realized she'd gone to sleep with her book in her hand. The light on the headboard of her bed was still burning. She yawned and stretched her arms back over her head. She didn't think of the problems in which she had been involved until she left for school. She ate hot oatmeal mixed with brown sugar and chopped dates and drank two glasses of orange juice while Wayne went over his poem three times.

"You'll do fine," Lois Miller said.

"That's what I think," Kathy said. "You know! I've

heard those lines so many times I think I can say them myself."

"Be my guest!" Wayne said. "Take my place in class."

"You coming home right after school?" Kathy's mother asked.

"Yes—No, I *won't!* This is the day we're to talk about a student council."

"Surely they don't expect to organize one yet this year. It's April."

"I don't know," Kathy said. "Just that we're to discuss the idea. I don't know what I think. How can I, when I don't know what we'd do—or what *it* would do."

"That's probably the purpose of this afternoon's meeting. To inform you, which is never a bad idea."

Chapter 10

The after school meeting lasted only forty-five minutes. The dean and assistant principal did most of the talking. As Kathy and Cindy walked home they decided that the idea of having a student council might be good or it might be bad! "I can see that it'd help the school know what students are feeling," Cindy said. "But a lot of kids would resent us."

"That's what I thought," Kathy said. "Either because they'd not be on the council or because they'd grouch at us about all the rules."

"I guess that's why they gave us these articles to read about what's happened in other schools—so we'd know whether we want to get into this thing."

"Do you have to do anything at home now?"

"Practice my piano lesson and help with dinner. Why? What's on your mind?"

"Nothing, except if I'm to help Carla I think I should maybe at least meet her ahead of time."

"Yes, you should, but tonight's a little soon. She came home this afternoon. Besides, I've decided to tell you what happened before you go. Carla's Mother helped me make up my mind."

"When can you tell me?"

"Let's see," Cindy said. "Tomorrow I work at the hospital until one. Then I take my music lesson. Wait one minute! I almost forgot. My parents have a Sunday school class supper tomorrow night. I could go, but even my father admits I've outgrown them. Could you stay with me while they're gone? I'd say all night if we weren't leaving early Sunday. The quartet my mother sings in is going down near Bloomington to the church where she grew up."

"I'm sure I can stay," Kathy said. "But—"

"But you have to ask. You'll call?"

"I'll call."

In a way Kathy felt a little lonely that evening, a little left out. *No one calls me like before. Cindy's busy and I plain don't know what to do with myself.*

"Are you too busy to run a couple of errands for me?" Kathy's mother asked as soon as she heard the back door bang.

"I'm not busy at all."

"For one thing I've neglected to take books back to

the library. They're due tomorrow. Would you rather wait until then?"

"No. Tonight's okay. I have something to do tomorrow. If you say it's okay for me to go to Cindy's—just for the evening."

"You sound—a little depressed."

"No, it's not that. I just don't know what to do. Cindy's *always* busy."

"I think I understand how you feel," her mother said. "I go through the same kind of time twice a year—when school begins and when it lets out."

"I don't understand."

"It's a change in the routine. We can't always adjust as quickly as we'd like. Of course, there might be another factor involved. Dependency."

"What did I depend on?" Kathy asked thoughtfully, "Oh, I think I see what you mean. I counted on Val or Pat to call me or ask me to go for a Coke or something when they didn't have anything else to do."

"You miss them?"

"*Could* I miss them and at the same time not want to belong to the group?" Kathy asked.

"Certainly. You could miss what they represented—approval, a kind of security."

"Was I ever wrong! Anything to eat?"

"Mrs. Wardelle gave me a dozen of her doughnuts for helping transplant her flowers."

"I'm surprised Wayne hasn't eaten them," Kathy said as she opened the plastic box. "He even left one dusted with cinnamon sugar. Where are the books?"

"On the hall table. You want bus fare?"

"No, I'd rather walk. The branch library's not that far."

As she waited for a car to pull out of a filling station someone called, "You lost, Kathy?"

She turned and saw Bill Grayson walking toward the row of gasoline pumps. "What do you mean lost? I live around here. You know that."

"Had to get your attention, didn't I"

"What are *you* doing here?"

"This is where I work," Bill said.

"You're not old enough to get a permit."

"I don't need one here. My dad's the boss. And I'd better get back to work. Business is big on Fridays."

Bill has a job and Cindy does candy striping. They're doing something useful, Kathy thought as she went into the library. *What was it Valerie called kids who work? Drones.*

The lady at the desk didn't even look up as Kathy put the books on the polished top of the curved counter. *Should I look for something to read? Might as well so long as I'm here.* After she'd chosen a biography and a mystery she waited to be checked out. When the librarian glanced at her card she said, "You must be Lois Miller's daughter."

"Yes."

"We went to school together. We haven't lost touch completely. I often think about the fact that she was the only person in our class who came to see me when I was in the hospital last fall."

I don't remember Mom going, Kathy thought. *Didn't she tell me? Or wasn't I paying any attention?*

"Is your mother all right?"

"She's fine. I'll tell her you asked."

As she reached the front door the librarian caught up with her. "I couldn't call out. I'd have disturbed others. But I suddenly remembered that we have a problem to which you might be the solution." She explained that high school girls came in three evenings a week and read to groups of children. "The girl who was to be here today is ill and we can't locate the others."

"Do you want me to do it?"

"Would you? Now I should tell you, there's no pay."

"That's okay," Kathy said. "I'll need to call my mother. Are the children here now?"

"They're coming. I'll go downstairs and get them corralled."

Kathy didn't have time to dread this new experience or worry about whether or not she could hold the interest of the group. She didn't even have to decide which book to read.

"This is the one the other girl had promised them," the librarian said.

The blue and yellow chairs were in a semicircle and all were filled except four. "Do you know how many will be here?"

"Not for sure. They have to register but don't always all come."

As Kathy sat down facing the group she heard quick footsteps on the stone stairs. She waited until the newcomers come through the door. "Kathy, what are you doing here?" Dina Conray asked.

"Are you going to be our story girl?" Doris asked.

"For today I am."

The hour went quickly. The children listened without much chair wiggling and with only one or two whisperings.

"I wish you could read every time," Dina said as they left the library.

"I think they have regular girls," Kathy said. "but I liked it. Say how did you girls get here? How are you going to get home?"

"Our mother brought us," Dina said.

"And our daddy will pick us up," Doris added. "We're supposed to sit right here on this bench unless it's raining."

"Which it isn't."

"Want me to wait with you?" Kathy asked.

"Please. Then you can ride home with us."

"Well, I can't do that, because I'm supposed to stop at the dairy store on my way home."

As she walked home with two books in the crook of one arm and the brown sack holding a carton of cottage cheese and a pound of butter in the other hand she wondered if she could become a regular story girl. *I liked the way I felt. Why haven't I thought about doing something like this before.*

As soon as she mentioned the idea to her mother she said, "Why not call Irene?"

"Irene?"

"The librarian, Irene Norman."

"Oh, I didn't know her name. Do you think this is something I should do on the telephone?"

"You can ask if you should. As soon as you've called, if you do, you can give me a boost and spread the frosting on this spice cake."

She thinks I ought to call, Kathy thought. *Because it's a good idea? Or because I don't know what to do with myself? Or both?*

"That was easy—easier than I expected," Kathy

said as she walked back to the kitchen. "I'm on the list now—as a substitute at first."

"That'll give you a chance to know if this is a way you want to use your time," her mother answered. "Sort of a trial run."

"I know I'll like it. I think I'll go over sometime to look at books and see what's new. Maybe I'll make a list of old ones—those I could never forget."

"That sounds like a positive move," her mother said.

Kathy liked the way she felt the rest of the evening. She didn't worry about all the bad things that happened. Thoughts of Val and Pat and Carla came to her mind but she didn't let them run around and around like records when the needle sticks.

"We going anyplace tonight, Dad?" Wayne asked at the table.

"Anything in mind?"

"Nothing much. Except Greg's Dad was going to take his sailboat out to the reservoir. There's a race Sunday."

"A regatta," Kathy said. "When it's sailboats people say *regatta*."

"I don't," Wayne answered. "I say race."

"You girls want to go?" Rex Miller asked.

"I don't believe—" Lois Miller began. "On second thought I guess I will—if you think some of the boats will be on the water tonight."

"Some may be making trial runs."

"You want to go, Kathy?"

"Yes. I like the looks of the sails. It's like the boats are one-wing birds."

Rex Miller parked near the landing and he and

88

Wayne walked down to the edge of the water. Kathy stayed in the car with her mother. The sun was still above the fringe of the trees on the horizon. Streaks of flaming color and layers of soft clouds filled the western arc of the sky. White sails edged across the breeze-rippled water. "What a lovely picture," Lois Miller said. "Almost too beautiful to bear."

"I feel like that sometimes—like when I hear certain music. We listened to a record at school in music appreciation class. I wrote down the name. It was Traumeri."

"I know that—a lovely haunting melody. We need more of that kind of music—less noise, more harmony."

Chapter 11

In one way I hesitate to make this suggestion,"
Kathy's mother said as the Millers ate breakfast the
next morning. "I don't want to begin something that
will be expensive to follow. How would you feel about
going shopping this morning for some new clothes,
Kathy?"

"Feel free to come right out and say what's on your
mind, Mom," Kathy said. "When that's what it is."

"When that's what it is," Lois Miller repeated. "Is
that a sentence?"

90

"If you get my meaning, it must be," Kathy said. "Is there any grape jelly left for my toast?"

"In the refrigerator," her mother replied. "You're up Wayne. Hand that jar to your sister."

"I didn't get up for grape jelly," Wayne complained. "I'm looking for those doughnuts."

"To the left. And if you put forth your utmost effort you might be able to carry a doughnut *and* the jelly jar."

"Do I have to go tagging along with you guys?" Wayne asked.

"Guys! Everyone's not a guy," Kathy said.

"You got what I meant. Do I, Mom? Have to go?"

"What would you rather do?"

"Almost *anything*."

"Well you could go to the store. Your father might find some errands for you to run."

"That's okay. And I like to look at all the things they sell—hinges and doorknobs and tools and stuff."

Kathy and her mother were in the stores for nearly four hours except for the time in the cafeteria in the mall. "You haven't tried to get me to change my mind about anything yet," Kathy said as they slid their trays along the stainless steel pole.

"Except to say we can afford only three garments, besides the shoes."

As they began to eat, Lois Miller said, "I bit my tongue to keep back some objections—especially when you were trying to decide between the bold plaid and the smaller check."

"You like the check. But why didn't you say so?"

"Well, I reminded myself of the way I felt when Mother took me shopping. We were different in

91

several ways. And it seemed to me I always wore clothes that would be better for her. *Her* taste showed in what I wore more than mine."

"What's the other reason?" Kathy asked as she broke apart her blueberry muffin.

"You're showing us that you're growing up by the way you've handled yourself this week. If you have the maturity to break the ties with the 'In Group' you certainly are capable of choosing a skirt and a blouse and a—whatever you decide to buy after lunch."

"Maybe so," Kathy said. "You know something, Mom? Something I'm sort of figuring out about myself."

"Such as."

"Like I'm not the same with everyone. Like I change, act as others act."

"Oh, Kathy! Many people do that. People who are much much older than you."

"Seems sort of weak to me."

"Your grandmother has another word for it. She says, 'Some folk are wishy-washy.'"

Neither spoke for a few minutes. Kathy could see the entrance and watched people as they picked up trays and silverware at the end of the counter. She didn't spot anyone she knew. *Not many kids eat here. And I might know where the "In Group" is—if it's together. Where was it Cindy said she'd seen them? Going in someplace close to school—where I've never been.*

"While we're on the subject of people going along with others I've noticed something else," Lois Miller said. "Most of us are at our best when we're with one or a very few. Especially young people."

92

"Young people. Why us?"

"I used to think it was because of lack of experience. For one thing, I noticed that talk was easier and more shallow and chattery."

"Chattery? Is that a word? You don't think that about us now? Why?"

"Because I've listened. Even children much younger than you have a special kind of wisdom—an uncluttered knowing."

"Uncluttered by what?"

"Resentment, or cynicism, or prejudice perhaps."

"You ever hear signs of that uncluttered knowing in me?" Kathy asked.

"Certainly. And you know something? I think adults are responsible for the fact that young people often don't express the best of their natures. Who wants to confide in someone who isn't listening or disapproves of everything and is overly critical?"

"Not me."

"Well, shall we go?"

"We'd better. I go to Cindy's tonight. Remember?"

"And there's that little matter of the weekly cleaning of your room. Remember?"

Raindrops splattered on the parking lot as they left the shopping center. The plastic pennants which were strung in a crisscross pattern over the area snapped and rattled in the rising breeze. Scraps of paper, candy wrappers, sales slips, and handbills skittered and fluttered across paths and under cars.

"I just love this jumper," Kathy said as she looked into the brown and white bag. "What did the girl say—what color is it?"

"Bittersweet."

"That's right. It *is* like the berries on the back fence at Grandmother Miller's house. After they crack open."

"That's after frost comes," Lois Miller said. She looked both ways before pulling on to McGalliard Avenue. "For a long time I thought bittersweet was only the name of the vine."

"What else is it?"

"It also means either a mixture of bitterness and sweetness, or pleasure mixed with sadness."

What does that remind me of? Kathy thought. *Seems like I heard someone say something like that. Or was it me? Maybe it will come back to me.*

Kathy took her new clothes to her room and spread them out on the bed. *I didn't do such a bad job of choosing even if I say so myself. The creamy blouse will go with both the jumper and the checked skirt.*

She had finished cleaning her room except for dusting the round sections of her brass bed when the telephone rang. "I'll get it," she called.

"Kathy?" Cindy said. "I forgot to tell you my mother has dinner fixed for both of us. Some of what she's taking to the carry-in at church. Chicken and noodles and butterscotch pie mainly."

"Mainly! Who needs anything else?"

"What time can you come?"

"All I have to do is finish straightening up my room and take a shower. Like an hour from now. Is that okay?"

"Anytime is okay with me. See you."

"What are all of you going to do tonight?" Kathy asked as she went to the living room.

"No plans yet," her mother answered as she lugged

94

the cord of the vacuum cleaner. "Why? Afraid you'll miss something?"

"Just curious."

"I doubt if any of us leave the house tonight except Wayne. And he'll be inside after dark. You getting ready to go?"

"Before long."

"Will you stop at the variety store and get me a spool of black thread? The hem is out of my suit and I don't have even a raveling to match."

Kathy liked to wander around in the corner store. It stocked so many different things that she wondered if the clerks knew what was on the shelves and racks and in the deep storage drawers. She'd bought paper doll books and suckers when she was small and hair clasps and sneakers when she was older. *I found the right color of head scarf to match my corduroy coat a few weeks ago—before we went camping.*

She lifted a spool of thread from the slanted tray and watched other spools roll down to fill the space. She turned and saw Pat coming toward her. *She hasn't seen me. I could duck behind this rack and go up the other aisle.* Instead she said, "Hi, Pat."

Pat stopped and rammed her hands into the pockets of her denim jacket. Kathy could see that her fists were doubled. They were bumps under the pale blue fabric. "Hello," she said.

"You all right?" Kathy asked without being sure there was a reason for the question.

"What makes you think I'm not?"

"I don't know. Just a feeling, I guess."

"Well, I'm not. But talking won't help."

"Especially not to me?" Kathy asked.

"I didn't say that. Talking won't help. Not to anyone."

What's the matter with her? Kathy thought as she paid for the thread and left the store. *I've never seen Pat down before. She's been mad and hateful a lot of times, but today she's different. But I don't want to think about all that now. Not for a while.*

Cindy's parents were pulling away from the curb when Kathy came within sight of the Masters' home. They sounded the car horn and waved when they saw her.

"Want to eat before I tell you why Carla's been in the hospital?" Cindy asked.

"What do you want to do? I'm not too hungry. Mom and I both ate lunch."

"Then let's go back to my room. I have to turn off my record player."

"Hey!" Kathy said as she walked through the door. "You've redone your room!"

"Haven't you been here since? No, I guess it's been that long. Like it?"

"Love it. This shade of red and the white looks like cranberries and whipped cream."

"That's what this shade of paint and fabric is called—cranberry. Want to sit on the bed or the chair?"

"I'll take the chair. I love the way the high back fans out like a white wicker fan."

"So do I but I can't see it when I'm sitting in it." Cindy kicked off her sneakers and sat against the head of the bed. "Before I tell you about Carla there's something else I want to say, Kathy. I've thought about this a lot."

96

"About what?"

"It's this," Cindy said. "After I explain things, when you understand—well, I hope we—you and I—never have to talk about all this trouble again." She went on to say that her mother had advised her to drop the subject. "She said that people keep things going by talking about them over and over."

"I sort of understand that," Kathy said. "Like today Mom and I went shopping. And I didn't think about these other things all day—well, not much anyway."

"Shopping? What'd you get?"

"A jumper, a blouse, and a skirt. But I'll tell you about them later—after you tell me about Carla."

Chapter 12

I don't know if you've heard or not," Cindy began, "that Carla and Valerie are cousins."

"Yes, I knew. Aren't their mothers sisters?"

"No. All this might not have happened if they were. Carla's mother is a sister of Valerie's father."

"He lives out in Kansas somewhere now, doesn't he? But how could that make such a difference?"

"Because when Carla told her mother some of the things Val *says* she does, Mrs. Trask wrote to her brother. And later she called him, or maybe he called her, I'm not sure which. Anyway, she wouldn't if he wasn't her brother."

Cindy said that there had been a lot of talk, first between Mrs. Trask and her brother, then between Valerie's parents. "What it all added up to was that Val's father said he was going to try to get custody if things didn't change."

"But they didn't."

"I know. But he was made to think they had. You see Val—well, if there was one thing she didn't want to do it was live with her father. He never gave her everything she wanted or her own way all the time."

"Could that have caused the divorce?" Kathy asked.

"It could have, I guess. Anyway he came here and they had a big family conference, only Carla called it a fight."

"Did Carla have to *be* there?"

"No. But her uncle talked to her. And when Valerie found that out she really persecuted Carla—did things to scare her into being quiet. She'd write ugly notes and call her bad names in the hall and even in the classroom. Once she drew a picture and taped it on Carla's locker. The girl had a big mouth and Val printed *Miss Loose Lips* on it."

"How do you know for sure it was Val?"

"Because I saw her. Pat was along and two or three others. They were laughing and saying mean things. I walked between Val and the others and reached out to grab the piece of construction paper. As I turned I saw Carla. It was too late. She'd seen. And she hasn't been back to school since."

"Oh, this is awful," Kathy said.

"Didn't you ever hear *anything* about this?"

99

"No. Like I said, I thought Carla had moved. Maybe I wasn't as far into the 'In Group' as I thought."

"Which is a good thing—as I see it," Cindy said. She went on to say that Carla had tried to hide what was happening from her mother. "She pretended to be sick and cried a lot because she didn't want to go to school. When the doctor found nothing wrong and she was told she had to go back to school, she began to tremble all over. She couldn't, just couldn't. That's when she went to the hospital."

"There's something I don't understand," Kathy said. "If the group was shunning Carla, why was Val afraid of what she'd say, if she wasn't hearing anything?"

"Probably because she'd heard so much and could be pretty sure of why they still met and huddled together. Carla's mother kept asking her questions like, 'Has the group broken up?' She was really under pressure."

I must be really stupid, Kathy thought. *I didn't ever think those girls did all the things they bragged about doing. Or did I walk away so often that I didn't realize as much as Carla did?*

"Say, I don't know about you, but I'm starved," Cindy said.

"Me too. But I'm thinking how I'd feel if I was in Carla's place. It would be hard, really hard for me to go back to school."

"It will be. But the counseling at the hospital has helped. She doesn't feel guilty about telling her mother now—because she was really worried about Val. Besides we can help her."

100

"That's the reason for me going over to do homework. Right?"

"Right. And we can stand by her at school. When you get to know her, you'll want to. Now let's eat!"

The girls filled plates and went to eat in the family room. They talked about the new city tennis courts, how scared they had been when the tornado warning was flashed on the television screen, and how awful Renee's cake tasted when she dipped into the wrong canister in home economics class. "Ugh, salty frosting," Cindy said. "I have to have another piece of pie to take that taste out of my mind."

"Some excuse! After we eat and wash the dishes do you want to go see my new things?"

"If it's not dark. We could leave the dishes until later."

"Whatever you say."

"Let's go, but come back soon."

As they walked down the steps Pat came around the corner of the house. "Just as I walked to your back door the light went out. Trying to give me the slip, huh?"

"No, I didn't see you," Cindy said.

"Well, maybe."

"No maybe about it. I didn't see you," Cindy said.

"You don't have to bite my head off. I guess it was dumb to come."

"I'm sorry," Cindy said.

"Well, I don't blame you much for not falling all over me. But I did want to talk to you. I guess you can't believe *that* Kathy. Not after the way I talked to you in the store."

"In the store?" Cindy asked.

"I saw her on the way over."

"And I said it wouldn't do any good to talk—not to anyone."

"But now you want to?" Cindy asked.

"I have to. Or explode."

"Come on in," Cindy said.

"I wouldn't want to keep you from going wherever it was you started."

"Just to see my new clothes," Kathy said. "They'll be there later."

Cindy led the way to the living room.

"If you came to see Cindy, I can go outside," Kathy said.

"No. I knew you were here. I watched you from the corner."

Kathy and Cindy sat on the coral and brown couch and Pat faced them from a tufted leather chair. "I'm getting some of the same treatment we gave you—you and a lot of other girls."

"Why? From who?"

"The *who* is easy—from Val. The *why* is harder to talk about. I'm not going to come out looking so good. Not that I ever did, with Cindy especially. It's all because I can't go to Barneys. My Dad put his foot down on that."

"Barneys? Is that where the group gets together now?" Cindy asked.

She didn't say 'In Group' this time, Kathy noticed, *just group.*

"Yes. Val picked it. And it's not too bad in some ways. The cheeseburgers are okay. But not what my Dad heard about what's sold from under the counter."

"I've heard," Cindy said.

I haven't, Kathy thought. *I surely don't listen as well as others.*

"I don't want to say what it is—or what people say," Pat said. "Val says I'm a baby, parent-tied. But I can't go. I'll never never get a sports car out of him if I do. No matter what Val says, I'll not risk losing out on a car. It's going to be an MG—bright yellow I think. Well, I'd better run."

"Why did she tell us all of this?" Cindy asked, as they stood outside the door and watched Pat cross the street.

"She probably feels lost. Dumped. I did a little. And Pat's been in the group a long time."

"Listen to us," Cindy said. "We weren't going to talk about all this."

"I know. We weren't until Pat came. It's nearly dark. We'd better not go to my house."

"No. Mother says the streetlights are too dim and far apart on this street."

Cindy's parents came home at nine-thirty and all three of the Masters family walked home with Kathy. The parents talked while Cindy ran up to see the new clothes. "We'll have to get together this week to plan the trip to Chicago," Lois Miller said. "Could you come Tuesday evening?"

"We'll be here," Cindy's mother said.

After Kathy went to bed she lay awake until after ten o'clock. *A lot of things are better, working out as Mom would say. But I still feel upset about Valerie. Or hurt? Or both? And I don't understand why she wants to hurt people—or boss them around. Does anyone?*

She tried to remember conversations she'd had with Valerie. *We weren't alone very often. There was one*

103

time when we walked to the downtown library together. She remembered that they hadn't planned to meet and Kathy didn't even know that Val was behind her until she had to wait for the traffic light to change from red to green. "You going uptown?" Kathy asked.

"No. Right here. Not—not for myself."

She doesn't want to say why she's at the library. That's funny, but I guess it's her business.

She was ready to leave when Val came to the desk with a stack of books. Kathy couldn't help asking, "Are you going to read all *those?*"

"No. They're not for me. My mother sent me. But she won't read them."

Kathy had been puzzled but didn't want to ask any more questions. Now as she stared at the illuminated face of her small clock she thought, *What did that mean? Why did Mrs. Harper send for books she wouldn't read. That doesn't make any sense to me.*

She doubled her pillow and pounded both sides and lay back down. She heard her mother's steps on the stairs and then a whisper, "Asleep, Kathy?"

"No."

"Did you have a good time at Cindy's?"

"Yes—and yummy food—dumplings, the puffy kind. And butterscotch pie."

"I don't know whether we've told you that Greg is going to Chicago with us."

"I guess that's fair. Wayne needs someone."

"That's what Wayne said," her mother answered.

"Don't you want to hear about Carla's illness?" Kathy asked.

"I know the basic reason. Cindy's mother told me while you girls were up here. Were you shocked?"

"Yes. I knew a little bit about how mean Valerie could be. But I never thought she'd go so far. Was I ever wrong!"

"It frightens me to think a girl from a family we've always known could be so vicious," Lois Miller said. "And I always thought she was one of the most popular girls in school."

"Maybe it depends."

"On what?"

"On what popular means—on what you have to do to be called *that*," Kathy said.

"Then, if that's true, popularity might depend on who's pinning that label on someone."

"It sure does," Kathy said.

"Does it really mean anything?"

"Not always anything good."

"Well, I'd better let you get to sleep. Even if tomorrow's not a school day."

Kathy reached out to the table and turned the knob to the FM side of the radio dial. The soft music made her realize how sleepy she was.

Chapter 13

Yesterday was truly a day of rest for me," Lois Miller said as she browned batter-dipped bread. "I was busy but not rushed. Sunday was, I guess you could say, the way it's supposed to be."

"What you mean," Rex Miller said, "is that it was the way it was when we were growing up."

"I suppose so. There was a regular pattern—Sunday school and church and a nice noon dinner."

"What did you do afterward?" Kathy asked.

Her mother brought the last two pieces of French

toast to her plate and sat down. "Well, I have to be honest. Now, looking back, the view seems pleasant. Actually, I was often very lonely—more than on any other day of the week." She went on to say that all the grown-ups took a nap if there weren't any guests. "And sometimes if it was only Aunt Mae or Uncle Arthur who ate with us they dozed too. So I guess there was a mixture of—what were we talking about the other evening? Bittersweet. The bitter and the sweet."

"What was sweet?" Kathy asked.

"Oh, being able to slip out and climb to the thickest limb of the plum tree or wander to the end of the garden where the grass was tall and maiden blush apples fell when they were mealy ripe."

"Didn't you have *anyone* to play with?" Wayne asked.

"Not often. There wasn't so much togetherness—which had its advantages."

"You people had better look at the clock," Kathy's father said. "This is Monday and not a day of rest."

Before Kathy left the kitchen she said, "Remember this is the evening I go to help Carla Trask. I'm not sure how long I'll be there."

"Do you dread going?"

"A little, mainly because I don't want to say the wrong thing. But Cindy will be with me this first time. That ought to help."

There was little time for Kathy to think about what would happen if she saw Val or Wendy. She didn't look for the members of the group in the halls on the way to classes. She was too busy to even think about them. The clerk in the office gave her the list of Carla's classes and before the end of the day she'd collected a stack of books and assignments for a week.

She met Cindy at her locker and they caught a bus at the corner. "Why a bus?" Kathy asked. "Doesn't she live close to us?"

"No. Why would you think that?"

"Well, her brother was riding his bike past our house one evening."

"Some kids roam around all over town. He might have been lonesome. Mrs. Trask was at the hospital as much as they'd let her be. Skip probably felt left out."

"Could be. I remember something Wayne said. He said Skip would be glad when his sister came home."

"It's funny," Kathy said as they left the bus and walked to Celia Avenue. "I can't picture her any-more—not very clearly."

"She's so pretty," Cindy said. "Her hair's sort of like copper—copper that's been spun into silk. And her eyes are really green—not gray like mine. Of course that's partly why Val wanted her in the group."

"What do you mean?"

"That's the kind they wanted—the prettiest, the ones boys would run after."

"Oh, Cindy. That can't be true. Look at me."

"I'm looking. So what?"

"Well, how can you say that's why I was included."

"You have to be kidding! Don't you know how beautiful you are?"

Kathy was embarrassed. "I don't think you are

The girls sat down at a table. "Oh, look," Kathy said. "I see a cardinal—two of them!"

108

seeing well. Must need your eyes tested or something. And another thing, boys don't run after me."

"Give them time! Here we are. This is where the Trasks live."

Carla met them at the door. "I saw you coming. Hi, Kathy. You going to stay, Cindy?"

"For a little while. I'm taking an extra music lesson this week to get ready for a spring recital."

Carla led them to a room at the back of the limestone house. Logs were blazing in the fireplace. Sparks flew as a log shifted. "It's not that cold but I love to watch the flames." She'd set a card table near the three wide windows.

"Is this all right?" she asked.

"It's fine," Kathy said, as she put the books and her clutch purse on the table. "Oh, look. I see a cardinal—two of them!"

"Yes. They have a nest somewhere near."

Before they began to work, Kathy said, "This is all makeup work. Your teachers said they didn't want to overload you. If you can do more in a week, let me know."

"Are you coming more than once a week?"

"Well, I've been thinking. You might have questions. You could call me about some of them. But how would it be if I came twice to tell what we're doing now—So you'll understand more when you get to where we are."

"I wouldn't want this to be hard on you," Carla said, "and take up too much of your time."

"Don't worry about that," Kathy said. "To tell you the truth, I think I've caught something from Cindy—the busy bug."

110

The girls mixed work and getting acquainted talk for over an hour. *It's a lot easier than I thought it would be. Carla's shy but sort of gentle—easy to be with.* After glancing at the clock, Kathy said, "I brought a list of things I did for extra credit, like reports. You can keep this."

"As she tore the page from her notebook someone asked, "Is it all right if I come in?"

"I kept thinking you would," Carla said. "This is Kathy Miller, Mother."

She's like Carla, Kathy thought. *Or the other way around. The hair's the same and the eyes, except that Mrs. Trask's are sadder.*

"It's good of you to come—and more so because you two weren't friends, before."

"No. We came from different junior highs," Carla said.

"Nevertheless, we are so appreciative."

"It's been fun—a good time," Kathy said. She looked at the wall which was centered by the gray stone fireplace. "I've never seen so many books, except in a library."

"Mother was a librarian," Carla said. She cataloged all those books just like at school and uptown. And she's read them all."

"That's why we have them," Mrs. Trask said. Then her face changed as she paused. She clamped her lips together and her eyes changed from green to gray. "But some people don't use them for that purpose. They only take them out of the library when they're having bridge club—to impress people."

"Please," Carla said. "Don't think about that so much."

111

She means Mrs. Harper, Kathy realized. *That's what Val meant when she said her mother wouldn't* · *read the stack of books.*

"I'm sorry," Mrs. Trask said. "I came in here to ask if you could stop long enough to sample my fudge bars. I tried a new recipe."

"We're finished," Carla said. "and I'm willing to test the cookies—as a favor to you."

She's trying to cheer her mother up by teasing her a little, Kathy thought. *I do that to Mom sometimes.*

The girls took the chewy chocolate squares to the patio outside the glass double doors. They sat in the long glider and talked as they rocked and ate. "What would you be doing if you weren't here?" Carla asked.

"Doing homework maybe. Or reading a book," Kathy said. Then she thought, "What Carla's really asking is do I have anything to do with the group now?"

Carla dug her heel into the fiber rug in front of the glider and shoved until the rocking motion was faster. "You know something! It feels good to be back to work again. I guess Dr. Schuller knew what he was saying when he told me I was ready."

"You asked me what I'd do tonight. There is something that might come up." She told about being on the list of story girls at the library. I could get called anytime."

"If you do, we can switch nights."

"No problem," Kathy said. "Well, I sort of hate to leave. But it'll soon be mealtime. Call me now!"

"Will do, and thank you so much."

The Millers had the first backyard cookout of the year that evening. Kathy saw heat waves shimmering above the charcoal grill as she crossed the backyard. "I may be rushing things a little," Lois Miller said as she molded ground beef into patties, "But it's been such a beautiful day."

The air was cooler by the time they finished the meal. "Want to get us some sweaters, Wayne?" His mother asked as she slipped marshmallows on the prongs of a long-handled fork.

"I don't even want to move," Wayne said. "Not after two hamburgers and the rest of the stuff. But I will."

"It's so clean and clear I hate to go inside," Mrs. Miller said. "Do you get a sniff of the blossoms on Mrs. Wardelle's clove bush now and then?"

"I do," Kathy said. "When the breeze is stronger."

Each of the Millers talked about their day and Kathy's father said he'd picked up the tickets for the Chicago trip. "How did you get along with your theme, Wayne?" Lois Miller asked.

"Better 'n I thought," Wayne said. "I found out something today—about myself."

"What was that?" Rex Miller asked.

"Well. I really strained my brain trying to think what to write. Then I made up my mind to tell about the time Grandpa Miller upset the beehive—when he rolled around in the grass because he was getting stung."

"Are you *laughing?*" Kathy asked. "That wasn't funny."

"You weren't there. It sure looked funny to see Grandpa turning over and over with that big wire bee hat sitting sideways. But I knew better than to laugh then."

"But what did you learn about yourself?"

"I'm getting to that. I had to sharpen my pencil before I could write a word. I'd chewed the lead just thinking. Then I got two sentences down and that's when I figured this out. While you're writing the first thing you think of the next."

"That's an important discovery," Kathy's father said. "I'd add that if you don't write the one thing you may never think of the other."

"I suppose psychologists or people who do behavior studies have a name for this process," Lois Miller said. "But Wayne's definition is full of wisdom."

"Better watch it, Mom," Kathy said. "He'll be getting the big head."

"You're just jealous because I thought of something ahead of you."

Kathy heard her parents' voices but didn't pay any attention to what they said for several minutes. *There's so much to figure out, as Wayne said. Like does Mrs. Harper's doing things for show have something to do with Val being cruel? She doesn't want to live with her father because she can't get her own way. But some things about staying here aren't so good.* She drew a deep breath. *If I was in Val's place right now I wouldn't see anything good. How* **does** *she feel?*

The wail of a siren came from the direction of Godman Avenue. *A police car or an ambulance,* she thought. *Is there a difference? That's like a lot of things I never noticed. Is this a growing up sign, to have questions about things you never noticed before? I'm not sure I'm ready for all this thinking.* She leaned her head on a doubled back arm. And the words, *ready or not you shall be caught,* drifted into her mind.

114

Chapter 14

Kathy worked with Carla again on Thursday evening and didn't get home until a few minutes before five o'clock. "I've really been busy this week," she said as she put her books on the kitchen table. "The librarian asking me to be the regular story girl on Wednesdays filled up my time."

"Are you complaining?" her mother asked.

"No, I like what I'm doing. What's cooking?" she asked.

"Irish stew in the crock-pot and corn bread in the oven."

"Do I have time to wash my hair before we eat?"

"To wash it, yes, but you may not be able to get it all the way dry. Need help?"

"I can manage. And I'll rinse it three times, so you don't have to remind me—not this time."

As Kathy worked the shampoo into a sudsy cap she thought about what clothes she'd take to Chicago. *Mom said to wear one outfit and take two. It'll be my bittersweet jumper for sure and maybe the brown turtleneck Grandma Miller gave me for my birthday. I'll have to think about what else. Maybe I'll call Cindy and find out what she's taking.*

She wrapped a heavy turquoise towel around her head, walked to the dresser and glanced in the mirror. *I look like someone from Arabian Nights—those guys that sat cross-legged and smoked strange looking pipes or coaxed snakes out of baskets.*

She remembered what Cindy told her of the reason Valerie had wanted her to join the group. She leaned over and put her elbows on top of the dresser and stared at herself, turning her head first to one side, then the other. *I don't think I'm that pretty. What did Val say once? That someone had boy-catching looks. I don't see anything so terribly bad about my face. But nothing so great either. I guess I'm used to the way I look. Even to the cowlick up there.*

"Admiring yourself?" her mother said from the hall.

"No. I was just trying to see if I could find out what Cindy meant." She told her mother that Val and the

"I don't see anything so bad about my face," Kathy thought. "But nothing so great either."

116

others wanted girls in their group who'd be attractive to boys.

"I guess that's another thing that hasn't changed."

"What do you mean?" Kathy asked.

"They had clubs when I was in high school—but only two of them. Some girls were on edge for weeks, afraid they wouldn't be on the pledge list. They'd die if they weren't."

"Were you?"

"I wasn't pledged. I had my bad time afterward when my mother found out I sent my bid back—that I'd refused it."

"Did she want you to belong?" Kathy asked.

"Oh, did she! Probably because belonging was so important to her."

"You didn't say *why* you didn't want it."

"This is something I kept to myself for years. The sworn to secrecy vow was a strong pressure." She said her cousin was in one of the clubs and had told what happened when new girls were being voted either in or out. "Reba said it sickened her to hear fine girls rejected because they weren't cute and wouldn't ever be popular. She'd argue when friends were being discussed and someone always said *she* didn't fit. After hearing that a few times she dropped her membership."

"Then the same things went on back then," Kathy said.

"To some degree," her mother said. "But from what I hear, I think it was easier for us to stand for what we believe. There were more of us. Well! I came up to choose what I'm taking to Chicago. Have you decided?"

"Not yet. I have to call Cindy first."

"That's another way teenagers haven't changed. My father sometimes said that I'd never have reached school if it hadn't been for Alexander Graham Bell and his invention."

The Millers were at the table when Cindy came to the back door. "I tried to call you," she said, "but something's wrong with our telephone. We can't call out, but people can call us."

"That's what I was going to do," Kathy said.

"Do you have a lot to do to get ready for the trip?"

"No, not after I decide what to take."

"Why?"

"Well, Carla called and wants to know if we'd like to go bike riding."

"Would she ride over here? That's a long way."

"Her father would bring her over—haul the bike in his truck. You don't have to go."

"Oh, I want to," Kathy said. "And it's great that Carla wants to go places."

"I know," Cindy said. "You'll come in a little while?"

"I'll be there. It's okay, isn't it, Mom?"

"It's okay. But be back before dark."

The three girls rode out almost to the end of Godman then crossed over and came back on Jackson. "This sure is a good way to dry my hair," Kathy said as they came to a four-way stop.

"It's just beautiful," Carla said. "Shining and black. You aren't thinking about having it cut are you?"

"Oh, I think about it. Especially when it's hard to get the tangles out. Natural curls aren't all that great."

As they came to the cluster of stores east of the high

119

school, Kathy saw an orange sports car pull into a slanted parking place. "That's like the one I saw Wendy Larrimore in one day."

As they rode Kathy saw Val and Wendy climb over the low door. *How will Carla feel if she sees them?* She thought. *Or what will they do if they see her—or us?* She glanced sideways at Cindy. *She's wondering how Carla will feel too.*

The light in the traffic sign changed to red as the girls came to the corner. "That's Val and Wendy," Carla said. "Is this where they go now? Barneys?"

"Yes. That's what I heard."

"Then let's go to the Sundae Shop," Carla said. "I've missed that place. Or do we have time?"

"We have time," Cindy said.

"I want a—what do I want?" Carla said as she slid into a knotty-pine booth. "It's a choice between a hot fudge sundae and a pineapple soda."

"No cheeseburger? No french fries?" Cindy asked.

"Not this time. My mother does them as well as anyone. But you know something, sodas and sundaes don't seem the same when they're not in the metal dishes and holders."

Several high school students were in the store but none were members of the group which had set themselves up as the most popular in school. A few freshman stopped to speak to the girls and two classmates said it was great to see Carla.

Kathy and Cindy discussed what they'd take to Chicago and decided on one dress-up outfit and two skirts with blouses or sweaters.

"You know something," Carla said. "If you two were going to be in school tomorrow I'd be tempted to go back."

120

"Aren't you supposed to ask the doctor?"

"Not exactly. He said I'd know when I was ready. And I do."

"But you will wait until Monday, won't you?" Cindy asked.

"Yes, I will. For one reason I still have a little makeup work to do."

"A little!" Kathy said. "You must have really worked."

Carla's father was waiting for her and the other two girls sat down on the top step which led to the porch. "I should go on home," Kathy said. "It's nearly dark."

"Not quite."

Kathy watched a bird hop along a low limb of the redbud tree in the corner of the yard. She remembered the evening she'd walked into the snowy woods and scattered scraps for the birds. *So much has happened since we were stuck out there in that camper*, she thought.

"What's on your mind?"

"I was remembering when we were snowbound."

"That was two weeks ago wasn't it?" Cindy asked.

"It seems much longer in some ways. Things have changed so much."

"Not for me," Cindy said. "Except that you and I are friends again."

"Well, they have for me," Kathy said. "I've learned a lot for one thing—about me and other people."

"Good or bad?"

Kathy pushed her hair back and hooked it behind her ears. "Both. I mean it hurt to realize how cruel Val really is. And it's sad to think how Carla was hurt."

"But she's okay now."

"That's part of the good—that and finding better things to do than wait for someone to call me. Like being story girl at the library and helping Carla. I guess it's sort of like my jumper. Life I mean."

"Kathy! Are you serious? How could life be like a jumper? I've heard it compared to a lot of things, like a road and a mountain railway. But not a *jumper*."

"We're even," Kathy said. "Who ever heard of life being a mountain railway?"

"It's in our songbook at Sunday school. 'Life is like a mountain railway. With an engineer that's—' " Cindy began to sing.

"You're kidding!"

"No, it really is a song and I can sing all the verses."

"It's not really like a jumper. It's the color I was thinking about. Bittersweet."

"I can see *that*," Cindy said. "Good and bad mixed."

"Yes, the bitter and the sweet," Kathy said. "Now I have to go. Mom said your parents will take us to the Amtrak station tomorrow so our car won't be parked there all weekend."

"I know. Are you excited about going?"

"A little," Kathy said. "But glad is a better word for the way I feel. Well, I'm heading for home."

"See you."

Wayne rode toward her as she came within sight of their house. "Did Mom send you to find me?"

"No, I was just riding. I wasn't even looking for you."

"How far you going?"

"Around the block. Dark will be here by then."

"Care if I ride along?"

"Want to race?" Wayne asked.

"No, I just want to ride with you."

"Okay."

He's a good kid, she thought as they turned the corner. *He does his own thinking better than I have sometimes. Maybe he won't get hurt as I've been. I hope not.*

As they turned the last corner before reaching home Wayne said, "You go on, I have go see Greg."

Why? Kathy wondered. *They wouldn't talk about what to wear.*

"You don't want me to wait on you?"

"No, all we're going to do is look through his sports books and pick out several to read on the train."

Kathy smiled as she rode home. *They're getting ready in their way. Same trip, same train, on the same track. Just different ideas of what's important.*

Dorothy Hamilton, a Selma, Indiana, housewife began writing books after she became a grandmother. As a private tutor, she has helped several hundred students with learning difficulties. Many of her books reflect the hurts she observed in her students. She offers hope to others in similar circumstances.

Mindy is caught in the middle of her parent's divorce. *Charco* and his family live on unemployment checks. *Jason* would like to attend a trade school but his parents want him to go to college.

Other titles include: *Anita's Choice* (migrant

workers), *The Blue Caboose* (less expensive housing), *Busboys at Big Bend* (Mexican-American friendship), *The Castle* (friendship), *Christmas for Holly* (a foster child), *Cricket* (a pony story), and *The Gift of a Home* (problems of becoming rich).

Mrs. Hamilton is also author of *Jim Musco* (a Delaware Indian boy), *Kerry* (growing up), *Linda's Rain Tree* (a black girl), *Neva's Patchwork Pillow* (Appalachia), *Rosalie* (life in grandma's day), *Straight Mark* (drugs), *Tony Savala* (a Basque boy), and *Winter Girl* (jealousy).

In addition to writing, Mrs. Hamilton has spoken to more than 1,200 groups of children in Indiana, Ontario, Pennsylvania, Tennessee, and Virginia, mostly in public schools.

"What's your favorite part in writing a book?" one young student asked.

"Right now, it's being here with you," she replied.

"The prospect of facing 80 fifth- and sixth-graders at the same time is enough to send many adults for the nearest exit," a news reporter noted, "but for Dorothy Hamilton it is pure delight."